Woundabout

Woundabout

Written by
Lev Rosen

Illustrations by
Ellis Rosen

LB
LITTLE, BROWN AND COMPANY
New York   Boston

Little, Brown and Company

Hachette Book Group
1290 Avenue of the Americas, New York, NY 10104
Visit us at lb-kids.com

Little, Brown and Company is a division of Hachette Book Group, Inc. The Little, Brown name and logo are trademarks of Hachette Book Group, Inc.

The publisher is not responsible for websites (or their content) that are not owned by the publisher.

First Edition: June 2015

Library of Congress Cataloging-in-Publication Data

Rosen, Lev AC.
  Woundabout / written by Lev Rosen ; illustrations by Ellis Rosen.— First edition.
    pages cm
  Summary: Orphaned siblings nine-year-old Cordelia and eleven-year-old Connor, accompanied by their pet capybara, go to live with their aunt in the strange town of Woundabout, where nothing seems to change.
  ISBN 978-0-316-37078-3 (hardcover)—ISBN 978-0-316-37079-0 (ebook)—ISBN 978-0-316-37081-3 (library edition ebook)
  [1. City and town life—Fiction.   2. Brothers and sisters—Fiction.   3. Capybaras as pets—Fiction.   4. Change—Fiction.   5. Magic—Fiction.   6. Orphans—Fiction.]
  I. Rosen, Ellis, illustrator   II. Title.
  PZ7.1.R67Wo 2015
  [Fic]—dc23

                                                            2014019162

10 9 8 7 6 5 4 3 2 1

RRD-C

Printed in the United States of America

For our parents

Chapter 1

Many stories have happy beginnings. Cordelia King, age nine, and her brother, Connor King, age eleven, knew this because they had often been read those stories by their parents before bed. Stories where little girls run through fields chasing butterflies and stumble on portals to wondrous places. Stories where boys and their fathers go camping in verdant forests. Stories where everyone is happy except that they haven't fallen in love yet, which never seemed like much to complain about to Connor and Cordelia.

Sadly, this is not one of those stories.

This story begins with Cordelia and Connor on a train, going to the town of Woundabout. They were heading there because they were going to live with their aunt Marigold, whom they had never met in person. They were moving in with their aunt Marigold because their parents had died, quite unexpectedly, in a large explosion on their capybara-training ranch. To lose their parents so suddenly and strangely made them feel as though the train didn't have enough air, and they rolled the windows down to feel the wind, which reminded them that they were still breathing.

Their parents had trained the capybaras—which are like very large guinea pigs with only slightly better table manners—to sniff for bombs. Capybaras can smell things better than bloodhounds can, and they enjoy having their bellies rubbed. Connor and Cordelia had been in charge of the belly rubbing. The explosion had happened out in the woods on the ranch, where Cordelia and Connor's parents hid bombs and rewarded the capybaras who sniffed them out first. One of the bombs had been faulty, a policeman had told them afterward. It had gone off when it shouldn't have. Cordelia and Connor hadn't really been listening, though. They had been leaning against each other, a scratchy blanket thrown over their shoulders as though they were cold and it was raining, even though it was warm and dry. They had shivered anyway.

All the capybaras had died as well, except for the runt of the litter, named Kip, whom Connor and Cordelia had been playing Frisbee with far away from the explosion. Kip had nestled between them under the blanket, warm and soft, and both Connor and Cordelia stroked his back without realizing what they were doing. Had they been asked how they felt, Connor would have said he felt as though he were being crushed under a huge weight, and Cordelia would have said she felt as though the world were suddenly empty of everything but a dull tan color. But even if they would have used different words, they felt very much the same, and they knew as much without having to say anything at all.

They had packed their things, and the police had closed up the house and told them that it was theirs but that they had to stay with an adult, and their aunt was their only living relative. The children had nodded. They hadn't spoken much. They remembered their aunt Marigold from the phone conversations they had and the presents she sent them every year. But she'd never visited, and they'd never gone to visit her. Once, when their parents thought they were asleep, they'd heard their dad say to their pop that they couldn't visit Aunt Marigold, because she lived in a weird little town and no one would be friendly there. The town was called Woundabout.

They took the train to Woundabout a few days later. It was an old train, with peeling wallpaper that had once probably looked fancy.

Cordelia sat on a bench staring at her photo album. Cordelia loved to take photos because they were a way of keeping a beautiful moment that would be gone the next second. She knew that the photo wasn't

really the moment, but it reminded her of the beautiful thing she had seen, and was a way to save it. She had many photos of her parents, which she looked at over and over, wishing that they would do more than just remind her of them. Or at least remind her more—she would look at the pictures and suddenly remember the way her pop smelled and then she'd feel sad because that meant she'd forgotten it. The photos weren't enough to remember everything about them. And she didn't want to

lose any part of them.

Connor sometimes looked across at her photos, but mostly, he stared out the window, watching the trees and towns and factories with tall smokestacks go by. Kip stared out the window with him. Sometimes, Cordelia would look up and take a picture with her camera. Ever since her parents died, she always wore it around her neck, except when she went to sleep.

They arrived at the Woundabout train station at the end of a midsummer day, the kind when the sun is low and golden over the horizon, or it would have been, except that it was raining. They stood under the awning on the train platform to stay dry.

Kip ran out into the rain and splashed in the puddles.

Cordelia and Connor let him play, because capybaras usually spend lots of their day playing in the water, and the train, for some reason, had not had a capybara-class swimming pool.

It was dark and cloudy, but they could see Woundabout, glowing from streetlamps and the light that came through the clouds. The rain highlighted the edges of it, pouring down the sides of buildings in silvery lines. It looked to them to be a very peculiar town.

It was on a cliff that went higher and higher as it also became narrower and narrower, as if it

were built on the wing of an origami crane. Streets winded and wound about as though someone had dropped a bag of them on the floor, and the buildings all seemed old, but different kinds of old, from different centuries, and no one had bothered to keep them up very well. Connor thought it looked like a city he might have built out of blocks years ago, as a child, with things just plopped down wherever there was room. Cordelia picked up her camera and took a photo.

"Those roads don't look like they make much sense," Connor said. "They're not well planned." Connor wanted to be an architect or interior

designer, or maybe a city planner; he wasn't sure. He liked how shapes made from wood and brick could come together to create a place people would think of as home. He liked how homes and streets, when organized right, could make a community. He played games on his smartphone where he built houses and cities, and had to manage pollution levels and power plants and monitor the water supply. He even had to make sure that the streets were well laid out so there wasn't too much traffic and people wouldn't get lost. But he could tell that many people would get lost in Woundabout. He thought that he would have to see a map. He had an app on his smartphone for that, too. He took his phone out and looked at it. The picture on the screen was of their ranch. It looked sunny and hot in the picture. He looked back up at Woundabout, all rain and shadow, and frowned.

He looked away from Woundabout and down at his phone. He opened his map program. It should have created a map right away. But all the map of Woundabout showed was a big green triangle—the cliff. No roads, no landmarks. Connor furrowed his brow. He thought maybe it was just taking a long time to load, but as the seconds passed, it didn't change.

"Look at this," he said to Cordelia. She looked over.

"Weird," she said.

Luckily, Connor had a program for making maps from scratch, too, so he opened that, and tried to start a map of Woundabout, from what he could see of it.

"Cordelia and Connor King?" asked a man with an umbrella who appeared out of the rain. Connor thought he looked as straight and narrow as a support beam. His umbrella dripped rain like a veil, so they couldn't see his expression. Cordelia wanted to take a photo of the rain coming off the umbrella, but she knew it was rude to take someone's photo without asking, so she just looked up at him.

"We are," said Connor.

"Who are you?" asked Cordelia.

"I'm Gray, Miss Marigold's butler. I'm to bring

you to her home. Here, let me help you with your luggage."

Cordelia and Connor knew they weren't supposed to talk to strangers, but now everyone but each other was a stranger to them, and so they decided without speaking to go with the man called Gray, because it was better than standing in the rain all night. They followed him and got into his old-fashioned black car and let him put their luggage in the trunk. Kip sat on the seat between them, still dripping.

"I hope you'll like Woundabout," said Gray, getting into the car. "It's a very special place."

Chapter 2

Gray drove them around the city in silence, and both children stared out the window, seeing more and more of the town—each

part weirder than the last. There were statues of hippopotami perched on the corners of buildings and reaching up like dancers. Some even had wings, like angels.

There was a broken glass house in the middle of a cobblestone square. There were several construction lots, empty, their half-built buildings glistening in the rain. There was a park with a sign that said CRUMBLES PARK, but it looked like an overgrown jungle, with dead vines and bare bushes everywhere, so they couldn't see past the fence. There was a statue of a woman in a mask, with her hands out as though she were holding something, but she wasn't. There was a store that sold nothing but veiled hats. There was an old movie theater that wasn't playing anything. But strangest of all, there were no people.

"Maybe it's the rain," Connor said to his sister. He knew she was wondering about the lack of people as well. They stared at the roads—water poured down the steep hill like small rivers.

"Yeah," Cordelia said, "no one wants to go out in the rain."

"The streets are very slippery in the rain," Gray said to them as he drove. "If you lose your footing, you can slide all the way to the edge of town, and then you'd have to walk all the way back up. So no one goes out in the rain." Cordelia's eyes went wide as she imagined sliding down the winding streets like they were a waterslide.

"That would be fun," she said.

Connor shook his head. "Stone is too rough," he said. "You'd get cut up."

"Oh," Cordelia said, disappointed. Kip reached his head over Cordelia's lap and sniffed at the window, but she pushed his head back toward Connor and crossed her arms.

"I'm sorry you had to arrive on such a rainy night," Gray said. "We do get rain from time to time, but when the air is clear, it's really wonderful. People come from all over to take a breath of our air. They say it's curative."

"Curative?" Cordelia asked.

"Healing," Connor said. "But they say that

about lots of places. It doesn't really mean any-thing except that the air is clean and smells nice."

"Maybe so," Gray said. "But we are a special town. I promise you that."

They rode in the car for twenty minutes as it went farther and farther up the hill. When they were about halfway up, they turned left and drove toward the edge of town, until they were nearly cliffside. Gray stopped the car in front of a large house with a very tall wall. It was dark, but the house looked white in the car's headlights. The house seemed to tilt forward as if examining the children, deciding if it wanted to eat them. Gray helped them out of the car and walked them under his umbrella to the front door of the house. It opened as they approached, and a woman stood there. They'd always thought she was younger than their parents, and looking at her face, they could tell she was, but she seemed older, frail and delicate like dried leaves or some-body's grandmother. She had loopy golden curls and arms as thin as sticks.

"Oh, you're here!" she said, clasping her hands together. "I'm so glad. I'm your aunt Marigold."

"Hello," said Cordelia, extending her hand to shake Aunt Marigold's. She'd been taught this was the proper way to introduce herself. But Aunt Marigold wrapped her arms around both of them. She felt as fragile as she looked, and as she hugged them she also seemed to back as far away from them as possible, as if she were really doing some sort of yoga pose and hugging them was just an accident.

"I'm so happy to meet both of you. Oh!" she said, noticing Kip. "Is this your pet?"

"This is Kip," Connor said. "He's our parents' last capybara. Now he's our pet."

"That is . . . interesting," Aunt Marigold said, her voice high and tinkling like broken glass. "I've never seen a happy parrot before. He doesn't look like a bird."

"Capybara," Cordelia corrected.

Aunt Marigold stared down at Kip a moment longer, and Kip smiled up at her. "Well, as long as he's house-trained, I suppose, then you should all come in!"

She walked into the house, and Cordelia and Connor followed. It was a big house, all white and shiny. The front room had white marble floors and a white marble staircase. There was a vase on a pedestal in the corner. The vase was white and gold.

"This is a well-made house," Connor said. He admired the ornate art nouveau details on the ceiling and above the doorframes. Art nouveau is an old style of design that Connor had read about in one of his books—it made everything seem as though it had grown into place, instead of being put there by an artist.

"It's been the same forever," Aunt Marigold said. "I'll never change it."

"Shall I put their things in the guest rooms?" Gray asked from behind Cordelia and Connor. Neither of them had heard him follow them in.

"Not the guest rooms, Gray," Aunt Marigold said. "Their rooms."

"Of course, miss," Gray said neutrally. In the light, the children got their first good look at him, but they found him hard to describe. He was a neutral man. He wore a neutral-colored suit and he had eyes and hair the color of which would best be described as "in between."

"They're just up the stairs. Cordelia, yours is on the right. Connor, yours is on the left." As the children headed up the stairs, they heard Aunt Marigold say in a low, half-whispered voice, "I think I'm going to make a very good aunt, don't you, Gray?"

"Yes," Gray said. The children noticed he said this *very* neutrally.

Chapter 3

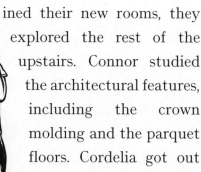

Upstairs, Cordelia and Connor looked at their new rooms. They were almost mirror images of each other, but Cordelia's had little flowers on the wallpaper, and Connor's had little birds on the wallpaper. After they'd examined their new rooms, they explored the rest of the upstairs. Connor studied the architectural features, including the crown molding and the parquet floors. Cordelia got out

her camera and started taking photos of things she found: there was a tree outside her window, the bath-room down the hall had blue and white tiles in the pattern of snowflakes, there was a ladder in the closet with flowers drawn on it, and Connor's room had an old metal vent in the floor.

They went back to Cordelia's room and sighed. There was excitement in exploring a new place, but it was starting to fade, and underneath was a familiar sadness.

"These sheets are soft," Cordelia said, sitting on her bed.

"They're very old," Gray said, appearing sud-denly in the hall between the two rooms. He brought the luggage into Cordelia's room and started to unpack, putting her things away for her.

"I can do that myself," Cordelia said.

"Nonsense," Gray said, smiling very slightly. "This is my job. Now that you

have seen your rooms, perhaps you would like to go downstairs for dinner. Your aunt is waiting in the dining room. It is just off the main foyer."

The children walked downstairs and through the foyer. The dining room they found themselves in was huge, but it seemed small because of the even huger chandelier that hung over the table. There was a fireplace off to one side, but no fire in it, which was strange because the house was chilly. Aunt Marigold sat at one end of the table, the top of her head obscured by the chandelier.

"Come and sit," she said. "Dinner is getting cold." The children sat on either side of her, where bowls had been laid out. Kip lay down underneath the table, waiting for the children to feed him scraps.

"What is this?" Connor asked, staring at the contents of his bowl.

"*Crème de carottes jaunes*," Aunt Marigold said.

Cordelia looked at Connor, as he knew a little French from studying architecture books.

"Carrot soup," he said. Neither of the children had any objection to trying new food, but somehow,

being so far away from home, with an aunt they'd never met before, in a house they'd never seen before, made them want the simple grilled cheese sandwiches and avocado that their parents used to make. They looked down at the soup and felt very alone.

"Could we light a fire in the fireplace?" asked Cordelia. She thought the roar and crackle of a fire might remind her of home, where they had a fire in the fireplace every night it got cold. The smell of woodsmoke always made her feel better.

"Oh, no," Aunt Marigold said. "It wouldn't work."

"We know how to use a fireplace," Connor said. "And how to clean the flue, if you need us to."

"No, no," Aunt Marigold said. "It's not that. It's just that fire is so difficult here. We use electric heat. Is it cold?" She looked past the children. They turned to find Gray at the other end of the table. They weren't sure how long he had been standing there. "Would you mind turning the heat up a little?"

"Not at all," he said, and left the room for a moment. The children stared down at their soup in silence, sad that they wouldn't get a fire.

"Tomorrow," Aunt Marigold said, "I'll take you to meet the Mayor."

"The Mayor?" Cordelia asked, playing with her soup. "Why would he want to meet us?"

"He wants to meet everyone who comes into the town. Everyone new. He's very hospitable."

Connor took one of the carrot chunks with his spoon and dropped it on the floor, where Kip gobbled it up.

"I hope you don't mind," Cordelia said, "but I think I'd like to just go to bed. It's been a long journey, and if we're meeting with the Mayor tomorrow, I'd like some rest."

"Of course, dear," Aunt Marigold said, patting Cordelia's hand. She didn't seem to quite know how to do this properly, though, as her hand stayed rigid and flat like a wooden spoon tapping a pot. She tilted her head, aware that something wasn't working, and withdrew her hand. She began softly patting her own hand, trying different palm shapes and rhythms, apparently hoping to discover the most comforting.

"I'll go, too," Connor said.

"All right. You know where your rooms are. I'll have Gray wake you tomorrow morning."

"Should we dress very nicely?" Connor asked. "If we're meeting the Mayor?"

"Oh, no. Just casual dress," Aunt Marigold said with a wave of her hand. "I'll be wearing something like this." She posed with her arms out, her silk dress gleaming and the gemstones in her headband sparkling.

"Um, okay," Connor said. The children swallowed. They didn't have anything as fancy as that.

After the children had gone to their bedrooms and changed into their pajamas, Connor came into Cordelia's room, where Cordelia was getting into bed.

"Can I sleep here tonight?" he asked. Cordelia nodded. She didn't want to be alone, either. They took the blankets from Connor's bed and spread them on the floor of Cordelia's room. Connor and Cordelia lay down on the floor, with Kip curled on top of them.

"So this is where we're going to live now?" Cordelia asked. The lights were out, but she knew

her brother was looking at her, so she turned to look at him, too, but could only see darkness.

"It's not such a bad place," Connor said. "It's a well-made house."

"I like the flowers on the wallpaper," Cordelia said, but she didn't sound very happy. "But this town is weird. Why do we have to meet the Mayor? What did she mean, fire is difficult here?"

"I don't know," Connor said. "But . . ." He thought for a moment, then went to his bag. He had a book of matches from home that he'd taken from their favorite restaurant. His parents had made him promise he wouldn't start any fires with it. The matchbook had a picture of a chili pepper on the front with smoke coming off it. He showed it to Cordelia.

"Maybe just the fire from the match will be enough," he said. "To remind you of home."

"Or . . ." Cordelia got up and went to where Gray had unpacked her things—she searched the dresser and the wardrobe before she found what she was looking for in the closet. It was a scented candle. Pop and Connor and Cordelia used to make them from scratch with wax and coloring and little vials of scent. This one was a mottled orange and gold, and it smelled like Pop's favorite things: oranges, chocolate, and wood. She brought it over to Connor, who smiled. He hadn't thought to pack a candle when they were leaving. He was happy Cordelia had.

He struck the match to light the candle. Nothing happened. He struck it again. Still nothing. He pulled another match out and struck that one—still nothing. He tried for what seemed like an hour, but couldn't even get a spark.

"I guess that's what she meant," Cordelia said.

"It doesn't make sense," Connor said. "How can a match not light?"

"Maybe it's the air," Cordelia said. "It could be too damp. Maybe that's why people say it's so healthy, like Gray said."

"Maybe," Connor said. "It's still weird. I feel like this town is keeping things from us."

"Me too," Cordelia said. "But maybe we can ask the Mayor tomorrow."

"Maybe," Connor said. "We should go to sleep."

"Yeah," Cordelia said. But both of them stayed awake for a long time, listening to the sound of rain on the window and Kip's snoring.

Chapter 4

The next morning, Gray walked into Cordelia's room to find the children asleep on the floor, wrapped around Kip. He nudged them with his foot until they awoke.

"Let's not tell Miss Marigold about this," he said. "Now get into your beds and I'll bring you breakfast."

The children rubbed their eyes and climbed into their beds. They left the doors to their rooms open so they could look across the hall at each other. Gray brought them trays with a breakfast of scrambled eggs and whole-wheat toast. They were very hungry, having not eaten much the night before. Kip ran between the two bedrooms, Cordelia and Connor alternating who gave him little bits to eat. The children smiled, watching him run frantically back and forth, trying to eat all the food as quickly as they offered it. They hadn't smiled in a while, and remembering this, they suddenly felt sad again.

As they ate, Gray cleaned up their blankets and opened their windows and expertly avoided being run into by Kip.

"Gray?" Cordelia asked. "Does Aunt Marigold have a computer? I was hoping to upload some of my photos and email them to friends back home." Cordelia's camera looked old, but it was actually a new camera in an old body—a present from her parents. They knew how she liked the filter the old lenses gave to her photos.

"Oh," Gray said, pausing, as though confused by the question. "I'm sorry, miss, but she doesn't have a computer. And the town doesn't have internet service."

"No internet?" Connor said, feeling an angry

mix of shock and disappointment. "How is that possible?"

"When the company that provides internet came around and wanted to put the wires in, the Mayor said no. He said they would make the town uglier."

"That doesn't make sense," Connor said. "The wires could go underground and they would increase the efficiency of the town. People would get things done faster."

"There's a post office in town," Gray said. "I can take you there to mail your letters. And if you ask your aunt Marigold, perhaps she'll let me drive you out of town to print out some of your photos. I think there's a place in the next town over that will do that. It's a long drive, though. A few hours."

Cordelia sighed. Connor's eyes were still wide with disbelief.

"Thank you, Gray," Cordelia said.

"Of course, miss." Gray took their breakfast trays from them as they had finished eating, and went back downstairs.

"I bet that's why my phone can't get a map of

the town," Connor said. "No local networks. I'd have to use the satellite feature, and I don't have the password. . . . Pop had it."

Connor looked down at his pajamas. Cordelia got out of bed and went over to him and sat on his bed with him, her head on his shoulder. Kip leapt up and joined them. They stayed very still for a moment, their bodies warm in the morning light that came through the windows.

"We should get ready," Connor said.

They washed and dressed and went downstairs, to where Aunt Marigold was waiting. She wore a long coat and an old-fashioned hat with a feather in it. The feather was pink and as long as Kip.

"Now remember," she said, "when you meet the Mayor, be quiet and stand out as little as possible. We don't want him to think you're going to cause trouble in our little town."

"Do we seem like we'd cause trouble?" Cordelia asked. She looked at Connor. He had one eyebrow raised. They both thought that meeting the Mayor and being treated like troublemakers was a little strange.

"Any new people can be trouble, if you're important like the Mayor," Aunt Marigold said. Cordelia and Connor both thought this didn't sound right, either, but they didn't argue. They didn't want to be trouble. "And your snappy llama can come in the car, but he probably should wait outside when we get there."

"Capybara," Connor said. "And his name is Kip."

"Right," Aunt Marigold said.

They all got into the car outside and drove to the Mayor's house. The sun was out, and Cordelia and Connor could see people in the streets. There was a man wrapping vines around a fence, and a woman walking two identical bulldogs. There was a mailman wearing a blue hat and shorts, and a woman in a fur coat raking a lawn. The people didn't talk to one another or wave. They all looked a little dreary.

Gray drove the car up through the town, to the very tip of it, where it ended in a sudden cliff and was so high that it was colder and the wind blew hard and fast. It was loud, too, and rang in their ears like police sirens. The children hugged their arms around themselves to keep warm when they got out of the car. The wind was so strong they felt as though they might blow away, and in fact they saw a few small rocks go sailing by. The children held on to the car and ducked when one of the flying stones got too close.

"Is this the famous curative air?" Cordelia asked loudly over the wind.

"Well, maybe it really forces you to breathe—whether you want to or not," Connor said back. "Hard not to take a big breath here." The children waited for Gray or Aunt Marigold to tell them more about the air, but they seemed not to have heard them.

At the very top of the city was a large house, with a larger plaza in front of it. From the plaza ran a swarm of streets, all racing downhill in different directions, and in the center of it was a manhole cover.

"Is this where all the streets start?" Connor asked loudly, to be heard over the wind. He thought it probably was, but that didn't seem like good planning to him.

"I don't know," Aunt Marigold said, holding her hat on her head so the wind wouldn't blow it away.

"Would the Mayor know?"

"Maybe, but don't ask him. Just be quiet."

"No trouble," Cordelia said quietly, exchanging a look with her brother. Something very peculiar was going on.

"This house is hundreds of years old," Connor

said, looking up at it. It was tall and wooden. On one side, there was a stone tower that was slightly bent over, and it was topped by a cone-shaped roof. The house made creaking noises in the wind, and there seemed to be music coming from inside.

The children followed Aunt Marigold to the door, while Gray stayed behind at the car, holding Kip's leash. Kip looked as though he wanted to run after them, but was held back by the strong wind, and as they watched, wide-eyed, he was blown into the air like a kite. They ran to try to grab him back down to earth, but thankfully Gray plucked Kip neatly from the air and held him under his arm as though nothing had happened. The children stared

at him for a moment, then turned back to Aunt Marigold, who hadn't seen any of this.

Aunt Marigold adjusted her coat and hat, motioned for Connor and Cordelia to stand behind her, and rang the doorbell.

Chapter 5

The door was opened by a young lady in a long black dress and apron. She didn't say anything, but just nodded and held the door open, gesturing down the hallway. She might have been keeping quiet because she knew she wouldn't be heard over the music that came booming out of the house. Connor and Cordelia didn't recognize the melody, but it sounded like a marching band. It had loud drums and cymbals, and felt patriotic.

Aunt Marigold walked into the house, and the children followed. Right through the door was a wooden hallway lined with tall framed photographs. The children looked at the photos as they passed, and they all seemed to be of the same man. He had a large nose and small eyes and hair that stuck out at all angles. In each photo, he was in a new place, doing something exciting. In one, he wore a fur-lined parka and stood on what looked like the top of a very tall mountain, with snow and ice everywhere. In another, he wore a pith helmet and stood in front of mysterious ruins in the desert, a palm tree to the side. In still another, he was underwater, in scuba gear, floating in front of a sunken ship.

As they walked farther down the hall, the music grew louder. They started to wonder if there might actually be a marching band somewhere in the house. The hallway came to an end after over a dozen portraits. There was a door here, too, and Aunt Marigold knocked very lightly on it. There was no response.

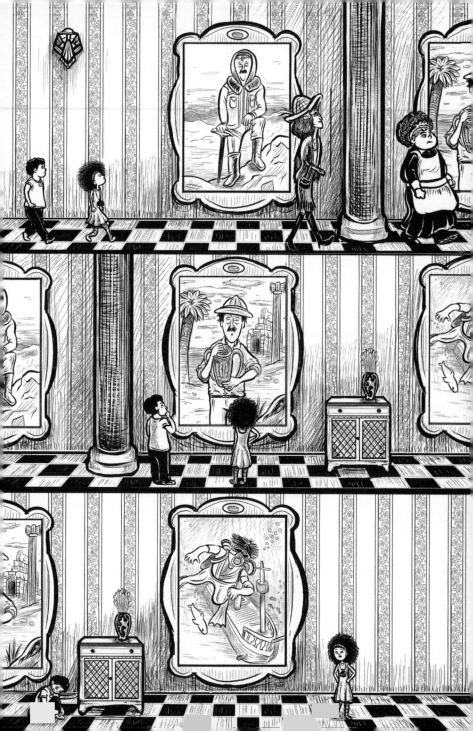

"You think he's been all those places?" Connor asked in a whisper, barely heard over the music. Cordelia nodded.

"They're real photos. And the same person took them all," Cordelia said as Aunt Marigold knocked lightly on the door again.

"How can you tell?"

"The way the photos are framed. Same style, use of light," Cordelia said. "She's a good photographer."

"How do you know it's a she?" Connor asked.

"You can see her in the reflection of his goggles in the underwater one," Cordelia said, pointing. "Right there." Aunt Marigold knocked on the door a third time as they studied the photo.

"Come in," shouted a bossy voice from beyond the door. Connor and Cordelia jumped, the voice was so loud and sudden. Aunt Marigold carefully opened the door and walked inside. The children followed her, tearing their eyes away from the photos. This was a big room, with a giant fireplace and blue carpet on the floor. All around the room were postcards, stuck to the walls with pushpins. They seemed out of place in the otherwise very fancy study. In front of the fireplace were a table and a sofa and chairs. A record player was on a small table against the wall, but next to that were speakers larger than Connor and Cordelia, from which the marching band music issued. The children resisted the urge to cover their ears.

There were windows that looked out on what seemed to be the very edge of the cliff, as there was nothing but ocean visible through them. The children wanted to run up to them and look outside, but they remembered what their aunt had told them and stayed where they were, just behind her.

"Ah, Marigold," said the bossy voice. It came from a man sitting on the sofa who had turned around when they came in. It was the same man as the one in the pictures from the hall, and the children assumed he must be the Mayor. He wore a button-down shirt, a purple tie, and tan pants, and was holding a mug of coffee. He spoke loudly, to be heard over the music, but acted as though this was normal. "Come sit down."

The children followed Aunt Marigold and sat in the chairs catty-corner from the sofa. Aunt Marigold kept her head down and her hands locked together, as though afraid to look the Mayor in the eye. Cordelia didn't feel the same way, though, and stared at him. His tie was covered in a pattern of masks, as if they were polka dots. He looked over at Cordelia and Connor and tilted his head to the side.

"Ah," he said, and blew on the steam rising from his coffee, "the new children." He said the word *children* funny, holding the *l* too long, as if he were skidding across ice. "I'm afraid this will have to be quick," he said. "The . . ." He paused, and looked at the children. "The *thing* went missing yesterday."

"Oh, no!" Aunt Marigold covered her mouth with both her hands. She was also speaking loudly, as though it were normal, instead of turning down the music. "How?"

"I don't know." The Mayor shrugged and furrowed his brow as though he wasn't used to saying those words and they tasted bad. "It was in the case." The Mayor pointed to a glass case by the window. It was open, and looked flimsy. "I'm afraid the window was open during the storm, and maybe the wind blew it out or . . . something." He scratched his head. "I can't think of who would steal it . . . but it can't fall into the wrong hands. I've created a search grid and I have teams out, but I'd like to go out and look myself."

"What thing?" Cordelia asked loudly. She knew she was supposed to stay quiet, but they were talking about something without telling her or her brother what it was, and that was rude, like whispering a secret in someone's ear in front of everyone

49

else. The Mayor turned his eyes on her and tilted his head again. The children started to think that this was what he did when he noticed something unpleasant, like gum stuck to his shoe.

"You like asking questions?" he said.

"They're the best way to learn," Cordelia replied. That was what her parents had always told her, but she felt as though maybe the Mayor would disagree.

"Ah, children, that may be true for school, but here in Woundabout, we don't ask questions."

"But then how will we learn?" Cordelia asked. The Mayor waggled a finger at her.

"That's a question," he said, as though very disappointed. Cordelia frowned. "But I'll answer it anyway, because you're new." He took a sip of his coffee and crossed his legs. "You see, if you have to ask other people questions, then you'll always be reliant on other people. We instruct our citizens in independence. We expect them to answer their own questions." He nodded, then looked away, out the window. "And if they can't find the answers . . . then they were never meant to know them in the first place." He turned back to the children and smiled the way they thought a hungry leopard might. "I'd ask if you understand, but that's a question, so I'm just going to assume you do."

The children stared at him in silence. Everything he'd said had made sense when he said it, but when they tried to think about it, it was as though his words had been thrown into a blender and mixed on the highest setting. All they understood was that they weren't supposed to ask questions.

"I like your house," Connor said after a moment. It seemed a safe thing to say. "It's very old."

The Mayor nodded at this. "It is old. Hasn't changed in years. Good eyes, son. Maybe you'll do in Woundabout. Just remember, no causing trouble, no asking questions. Things are the way they are because people older and smarter than you decided that was the best way for them to be. That's the rule of this town."

"Do you mean you?" Cordelia asked. She was getting really tired of the Mayor and his oily arrogance.

"More questions," the Mayor said. He turned a

little pink and shook his head and looked as though he was going to say something, but Aunt Marigold spoke first.

"They're very good children. Quiet. Won't cause any trouble or try to change anything." Her voice fluttered like a bird.

"What would we try to change?" Cordelia asked. The Mayor looked at her, his eyebrows getting closer and closer together.

"Their names are Connor and Cordelia. Isn't that sweet," Aunt Marigold interrupted. "They are just children, Mayor. . . ."

Suddenly the record scratched and the music went dead. Then the children understood why it was being played; the sound of the wind flooded over them, a loud, terrifying howling that seemed to come from everywhere. They heard how the windows rattled and the house creaked like nasty laughter. The Mayor stood and put down his mug, went over to the record player, and set the needle back on the record. The music started up again. It still wasn't nice to listen to, but it was less scary than the sound of the wind.

The Mayor returned to the sofa, leaned back in it, and took a long breath.

"I think that will do, Marigold," he said after a moment. "They're fine for now. Take them home, find them a routine. We'll see how it goes. I have to go tell people where to search now. So hurry, hurry." He waved them away with both hands, as if they were insects he was trying to shoo out of the room.

Aunt Marigold stood and took the children's hands, practically dragging them off their chairs, and led them back out through the hallways and into the car, where Kip jumped onto Connor's lap, then onto Cordelia's, and then back again. Aunt Marigold sat between them and took a long, heavy breath.

"That could have gone better," she said. "But it wasn't so bad. Gray, let's go home."

Chapter 6

At home, Aunt Marigold looked at the children and blinked a few times.

"What are we going to do now?" Connor asked.

"Remember what the Mayor said," Aunt Marigold replied. "No questions."

"But—" Cordelia started to say, then closed her mouth. She had been about to ask a question.

"Normally, this time of day, I read in bed. I have a routine. You children should have a routine, too."

"I'd like to visit the park we drove past last

night," Cordelia said. "Kip needs to get out. And he needs to swim, too."

"That sounds like a nice routine for you. Going to the park every afternoon."

"Well, not if it's raining," Connor said. "Also, I want to map the town."

"Oh, you shouldn't do that," Aunt Marigold said.

"Why not?" Connor asked, then looked down, realizing that was a question. Aunt Marigold looked at him blankly, apparently too befuddled by the question to realize it was a question.

"I just don't think you should," she said, which the children knew meant she didn't have a good reason. "As the Mayor said—don't ask questions. Go discover the answers." She said this as though she didn't quite believe it herself. The children looked at each other and rolled their eyes.

"I'll escort them to the park," Gray said. "I usually go there to read my paper before doing the daily shopping. It will only be the tiniest shift in my day. Not really a change at all."

"That sounds ideal," Aunt Marigold said, and

suddenly smiled brightly. "And, though you shouldn't map it, I don't see why Gray can't point out interesting things to you along the way to the park. He's the ideal tour guide. He knows the town perfectly. He was almost Mayor."

"Almost?" Cordelia asked, then covered her mouth, thinking she would be lectured for asking a question.

"There was an election," Gray said neutrally. "I lost. But I do know the town and love it. I grew up here. I'd be happy to point things out to you."

Connor and Cordelia wanted to ask why he'd lost the election, but that would be another question, so they held their tongues.

"I'll get my Frisbee and notebook," Connor said.

"And I'll get Kip's chew toy, so he doesn't try to gnaw on the benches," Cordelia said. Capybaras' teeth are constantly growing, so they have to chew things to keep them from getting too long. The children ran upstairs and grabbed their things. When they came back down, Aunt Marigold was already gone, presumably reading in her bed. But Gray was waiting for them at the door.

"Are you ready?" he asked. The children nodded.

Outside was warm and sunny, with a breeze that kept the day from getting too hot. Gray led them down twisty streets, pointing out people they passed.

"That's Mr. Thizzle. He walks his dog, Nosey, every day at this time. And there's Mrs. Washburn. She'll be hanging her laundry out to dry soon. Hello, Mrs. Washburn."

Mrs. Washburn started to wave at Gray but paused when she saw the children.

"These are Cordelia and Connor," Gray said. "Marigold's niece and nephew, come to stay with her."

"They're new!" Mrs. Washburn said, looking as

bewildered as she would have if a family of geckos had emerged from her laundry basket and begun singing in four-part harmony.

"Yes," Gray said.

"Oh," Mrs. Washburn said. She looked frightened of the children. Maybe, they thought, it was Kip. Not many people had seen a capybara before.

"This is Kip," Connor said. "He's harmless. He's a capybara." Mrs. Washburn said nothing, but kept staring.

"They have a great sense of smell," Connor said. Mrs. Washburn nodded, and turned away from them, back to her laundry, which, thankfully, was gecko-free. Cordelia took a photo of the way the clothes blew in the breeze.

Connor entered the streets and buildings on his smartphone, and Cordelia took photos of everything interesting that she saw. Gray didn't scold them for either of these things. In fact, he seemed almost happy with them—though they couldn't be sure. He was difficult to read.

Walking was different from driving through the city. They noticed that the streets were paved with cobblestones worn as flat as mirrors, and that there were manhole covers at every intersection with the word VOTE carved into them. Connor and Cordelia thought this was an odd, but probably very effective, way of reminding pedestrians to participate in the democratic process.

Gray walked ahead of them, pointing out buildings and saying what they were: "That's Mrs. Helmsley's Hat Shop," he said, nodding at the milliner's they'd seen when driving in. "And that used to be the museum, but the Mayor closed it." It was a wide building with statues of a hippo on

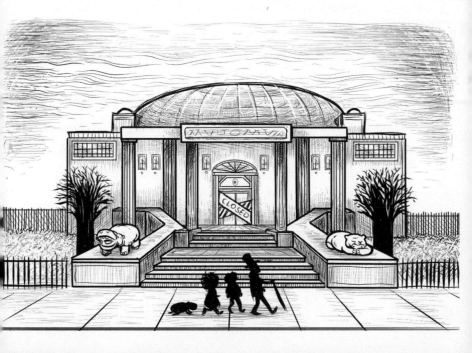

either side of the steps leading to the barred door. One hippo was sleeping. "The library is back that way," Gray said, pointing down a street, "but it's closed, too. Oh, this is Mr. Levin's Bakery."

"Were you really almost Mayor?" Connor asked suddenly. He knew he wasn't supposed to, but the question just popped out. But Gray didn't seem to mind at all.

"I was," Gray said. "Almost. But I lost the election, and so I'm not."

"But then, why are you Aunt Marigold's butler?" Cordelia asked. Gray stopped walking suddenly and opened his mouth, then closed it again, like a fish.

He opened his mouth again and said, "Your aunt Marigold is an extraordinary woman. I'm proud to work for her. And besides, there's not much difference between being a private servant or a public one." He looked down at them, and his lips curled into something that might have resembled a smile but which the children could tell was just pretending. "Anyway, let's get to the park. We can talk more there." He started walking faster,

and stopped pointing out shops, making Connor and Cordelia wonder if they'd hurt his feelings.

They passed through the square with the statue of the masked woman with her hands out. She was the size of a real person, and on a pedestal about as tall as a bench. Cordelia took a picture.

"Look," she said. "There's a hole in her back." Connor looked to where she was pointing, and indeed, there was a strange, eight-sided hole in the woman's back. It was about the size of his fist, and lined in metal. Kip sniffed at it curiously.

"Maybe she used to have wings," Connor suggested. Cordelia shrugged and took a photo.

"Come on, children!" Gray called, waiting at the edge of the square.

They walked farther along, and passed over a bridge. The water underneath it didn't seem to

run at all, and was a dark green color. Connor drew the river in his map.

"Why is the river so still?" Cordelia asked. She knew she wasn't supposed to ask questions, but Gray hadn't seemed to mind yet.

"The water in our town is sluggish," Gray said. "It used to be a fierce, roaring river."

"What changed it?" Connor asked.

"The water wound down," Gray said.

"Wound down?" Connor asked. "Like, dried up?"

"I suppose," Gray said, tilting his head.

"Hey, look—another hole," Cordelia said, pointing at another eight-sided hole, this one just beside the river.

"Weird," Connor said. "I'll start marking them down on my map." He drew a little dot next to the river on his map, and another on the statue in the square.

They continued onward until they came to the park they had passed last night. CRUMBLES PARK said the sign over the arch. The vines were wrapped all over the

gate, but Cordelia and Connor pulled it open with just a little difficulty. Then they walked into the park.

It was empty and barren. There were trees, but they had no leaves or flowers on them. There was grass, but it was short and occasional, not like a carpet, but like a man going bald. There was a pond, too, with a statue in the middle of it that looked like a fountain, but no water poured from it, and the pond was black and motionless.

"Well," Connor said. "I guess it will have to do."

Chapter 7

Kip splashed around in the pond. He didn't
seem to mind that the park wasn't really a
park so much as it was dirt with some dead
trees. Cordelia took photos of the trees, but they
weren't very inspiring or beautiful.

"It's summer," Connor said. "This place should
be green!"

"It's always like this," Gray said, sitting on the
one bench in the park, under a large, leafless tree.

"Isn't there a gardener or someone to plant
things?" Connor asked.

"There was once," Gray said. "But the Mayor

fired her." He took out the newspaper he had brought, which the children noticed was a week old and from another town, and began to read it. The children walked away to explore the park, staring at the rocks and the mud in the pond. Gray stayed on his bench, a reassuringly neutral pillar by the gate.

"So, what do you think the 'thing' the Mayor lost is?" Cordelia asked Connor, staring at a hand-sized patch of brown grass.

"I don't know," Connor said. "But I don't think the storm could have opened a box and taken a thing out the window."

"Maybe it's something from one of his travels," Cordelia suggested.

"Maybe," Connor said, sitting on his haunches and picking up an old stick from the ground. He started absentmindedly sketching building plans in the dirt. "But then why would Aunt Marigold care about it?"

"If it's really valuable," Cordelia said. "Maybe it's like a big jewel and everyone loves to see it, 'cause it's so beautiful."

"Maybe . . ." Connor said. He'd drawn a blueprint

of their old home—the ranch—without realizing it. He stood and erased it with his foot.

"Well," Cordelia said, putting her hands on her hips, "I think we should do just like the Mayor said."

"You do?" Connor said, looking over at her skeptically.

"Yes," Cordelia said. "He said we don't ask questions—we find out answers for ourselves. So let's do that. Let's find the thing."

"We don't know where it is, or what it is, or how it even went missing," Connor said.

"So we'll figure it out," Cordelia said. "We know the thing can't be bigger than Kip, because that was about the size of the box."

"And it can't be too heavy, if they think the rain could have blown it away." Connor nodded.

"So, we have a start. We'll just keep our eyes peeled for anything valuable-looking. He said it couldn't fall into the wrong hands—so maybe something dangerous-looking."

"Maybe it's an old sword from a Mayan temple," Connor said. They started walking along the border of the dead trees.

"Or a gun from a pirate ship," Cordelia said. She kicked at a pebble in front of her. "Or maybe it's something that has to do with why the town is so weird—the air, or why we can't light matches."

"Like . . . a magical humidifier?" Connor asked. He was a bit older, and didn't really believe in magic. "I don't think so. But maybe, like, an old stone that they say gives the town its good air. It wouldn't be real, of course, but something symbolic."

"Yeah," Cordelia said. "A magic rock that makes the air super curative." She did believe in magic. "We're new here. We'll notice things that people who live here walk right by, because it's all new to us."

"Like those weird little holes," Connor said.

"Look," Cordelia said to Connor, "there's another one!" They both looked down at the new hole Cordelia had found. This one was just in the grass, under a tree.

"What are they?" Cordelia asked. "Drainpipes?"

"No," Connor said. "That wouldn't make any sense. Why would one be in the back of the statue?

They don't need to drain." He stuck his hand into the hole. Inside, he could feel it was lined in metal until the bottom, about a foot down, where there were some gears and a slot. "It seems like it's mechanical."

"Maybe the city used to have signposts, or lamps? Or maybe mechanical statues that moved?"

"That would be something to see," Connor said. "But I don't know. Whatever it's part of is gone now."

Cordelia snapped a photo of the hole, then shrugged. "I wonder why they took it down," she said.

"Maybe the fountain or statue was asking too many questions," Connor said. Cordelia smiled at that.

"They're not all over," said a voice. Connor and Cordelia turned around. There was another boy standing there, as though he'd been watching them for a while. He looked to be around twelve, maybe thirteen—just a little older than Connor. "They're just in a few places. So it wasn't, like, statues or anything. That's daft." He held his shoulder slouched behind him, as if he was always bored. He reminded Connor and Cordelia of photos of rock stars or movie stars when they were

just walking on the street. And he talked as if he knew everything, but without being snobby. He was *cool*.

"Oh," Cordelia said. "I guess."

Connor and Cordelia looked at each other, not sure who this new person was.

"So you're the new kids," the boy said. "Everyone is talking about you."

"Who's everyone?" Connor asked.

"The town—people said you'd be moving here a few days ago, but no one believed it. They whispered about it over the fences in their backyards, but then you showed up, and now they're all shouting over the fences. No one moves into Woundabout. My parents have been asking the Mayor to let us move here for a year now, and he keeps saying later, but you two just get to move on in, no problem."

"Our parents died," Cordelia said. "We didn't have anywhere else to go."

"Oh." The boy's face softened. "I didn't know that." He stepped forward and held out a hand to shake. His hands were covered in dirt. "I'm Nico," he said. "My parents live down by the train station just outside town, but we come into Woundabout most days to deliver the vegetables and fruit we grow in our greenhouses to the store here."

"I'm Connor," Connor said, shaking Nico's hand, "and this is Cordelia."

"Why do your parents have to ask permission to move into the town?" Cordelia asked, shaking Nico's hand.

Nico shrugged. "Dunno. But it's the rule. The Mayor has to let people move in. My parents moved to just outside town a year ago, and have been begging the Mayor to let us move in ever since."

"Why here, though?" Cordelia asked. "It's kind of a weird place."

"My dad says the air on the cliff will be good for my sister. She's kinda sick." Nico rolled his eyes, as though he thought this was a dumb reason for wanting to move anywhere. Connor and Cordelia weren't sure what to say.

"Anyway," Nico said, "I'm gonna dash. Good meetin' you, though." He waved at them.

"Didn't you just get here?" Connor asked.

"Yeah, well," Nico said, turning and walking away. "I like it when it's less crowded."

He walked out the gate of the park, leaving Connor and Cordelia to stare after him.

"I guess he didn't like us," Cordelia said, folding her arms.

"At least we know there are some other kids nearby," Connor said. "We haven't seen anyone else."

"Yeah," Cordelia said. "So what do you want to do now?"

"Play with Kip?" Connor said.

Cordelia looked at Kip and narrowed her eyes. "No," she said.

"Why not?" Connor asked. Cordelia hadn't been mean to Kip lately—not exactly. But she used to love playing with him, and now she seemed to be going out of her way to ignore him.

"This park is boring," Cordelia said, kicking at the dirt. Connor nodded in agreement. "Maybe Gray will play with us," she said, and headed over to where Gray was sitting on

74

the bench, reading the newspaper. The children sat on the bench on either side of him. Kip lay down in the dirt in front of them.

"Something the matter?" Gray asked.

"This park is boring," Cordelia said again.

"It's just that it's so dead," Connor said. "Why do you come here every day?"

"I suppose it is barren," Gray said. "It used to be beautiful; the trees here, when they bloomed, were so full of petals they would explode like fireworks. They don't grow anywhere else in the world."

"They don't really grow here, either," Cordelia said.

"No," Gray said, folding his paper and putting it in his lap. "I guess not."

"So why do you come here every day?" Connor asked again. "Doesn't it make you sad to look at it and remember what it used to look like?"

"No," Gray said. He tilted his head. "Well, maybe a little. But it makes me happy, too, to remember it. And who knows—maybe one day it'll bloom again."

"That would take a really good gardener," Cordelia said.

"Landscaper," Connor corrected. "For a job this big, you'd need a whole team of landscapers."

The children looked out at the park of dust and bark and tried to imagine it alive again, but it was so dull they couldn't.

"Hey," Cordelia said, suddenly realizing something. "You answered our questions."

"Of course I did," Gray said.

"But the Mayor said we shouldn't ask questions," Connor said.

"Well, when you're with me, and no one else is around, you can ask me whatever you'd like," Gray said. "I don't mind. But I may not have the answers."

"Thank you," Connor said.

The children looked over Gray's lap at each other, trying to think of what to ask him. When they weren't supposed to ask questions, they had hundreds of them, but now that they were allowed, it seemed as though all the questions had run away.

"How did you meet Aunt Marigold?" Connor asked after a while. It seemed polite to ask Gray a question about himself.

"Oh, well, back when I was running for Mayor, I also had a different job. I was the town's only cab-driver. That's what I was doing when she moved here," Gray said, leaning back. "And so she hired me to pick her up from the train station with all her things. I had a different car back then, an old taxi, and with all her things, and steep roads leading up to her new house, the taxi couldn't handle it, and the engine gave out. But your aunt Marigold, you know, is an expert with cars—"

"She is?" Cordelia interrupted. "But she doesn't even drive."

"You shouldn't interrupt," Connor said.

"Sorry," Cordelia said.

"And there was that time when Dad's truck broke down and he called Aunt Marigold, and she told him how to fix it," Connor said.

Cordelia shook her head. She didn't remember, and the fact that there was something about their parents that Connor could remember and she didn't suddenly made her feel very sad, like looking at a family photo and seeing yourself cut out of it.

"Oh," Connor said. "Sorry. It must have been when you were still a baby."

"That's okay," Cordelia said. "It's not your fault." She took a deep breath. "Gray, will you finish your story? Sorry we interrupted."

"I don't mind," Gray said. "I forget how little you know of your aunt. There's not much more to the story, though. We got out of the car, and we fixed it together. She was impressed by how much I knew about cars and I thought she was one of the finest people I'd ever met. When we fixed the car

and got her stuff home, she asked me to work for her. I said yes. There wasn't much business in taxi driving."

"Do you like working for her?" Cordelia asked. "Is she nice?"

"I enjoy it very much. Your aunt is very nice. She just worries a lot. You don't know anything about her?"

"She sent us presents for our birthdays every year," Cordelia said. "She sent me a fish-eye lens for my camera."

"And we talked on the phone around Thanksgiving," Connor said. "She always said she hoped we'd come visit her."

"But she never visited," Cordelia said. "And Dad and Pop said we didn't visit her because it was so far away."

"Once, when they thought we were asleep, I heard Dad say she lived in a weird little place and no one would like us there," Connor said. Cordelia nodded.

"Well, I like you," Gray said. "And your aunt Marigold does, too."

The children nodded and looked at each other, wondering if it was enough to just have Gray and Aunt Marigold like them, or if they needed more.

"How does Aunt Marigold know so much about cars when she doesn't drive?" Cordelia asked, the question suddenly popping back into her head.

"Oh, but she used to drive," Gray said. "She was one of the best race car drivers in the world—and she built not just her race car, but the cars of some of the other best racers in the world, too."

"Really?" Connor asked. Both children found this hard to believe. "When?"

"Before you were born," Gray said. "Her car was called the *Careful Catapult* because even though she went so fast that it was like she flew out of a catapult, she never got into any accidents. She won several trophies."

"Why did she stop racing?" Cordelia asked.

"Ah," Gray said. "That's the sad part of the story."

"You can tell us," Connor said. "We know about sad stories."

"I suppose you do." Gray nodded. "Well, she had

a boyfriend, another race car driver, named Benny Banai. They called him Benny the Boom because he broke the speed of sound a few times, which creates a loud pop they call a sonic boom. He and your aunt raced against each other, and sometimes she won and sometimes he won, but even though they competed, they still loved each other very much and worked on each other's cars. But Benny wasn't as careful as your aunt. He made a modification to his car to make it go faster, but Marigold told him not to—she said it was too dangerous. They had a fight about it, and then he drove off to try out his new car. It flipped in the air ten times when he tried to turn, and crashed. They rushed him to the hospital, and Marigold stayed at his bedside for a week, but even with all the operations he never woke up." Gray paused and looked at the children, as if afraid to continue. He licked his lips slightly. "He died without ever waking up. After that, she stopped driving and moved to Woundabout."

Connor and Cordelia said nothing to each other, but they were thinking the same thing: their aunt had lost someone, just as they'd lost their parents.

And she'd lost a brother, their father. She knew what they were going through—sort of. That made them feel a little less lonely, but also sad for their aunt. And it made them wonder if they were going to grow up to be just like her.

"That's so sad," Cordelia said after a moment.

"It's a very sad story," Gray said. "But your aunt has dealt with Benny's death every day, and bit by bit, she's gotten less sad. She's certainly very happy now that you're here."

"She is?" Cordelia asked. "It feels like she doesn't know what to do with us, and with all the rules. Like we're making her life harder."

"You might be right," Gray said, looking up at the sky, "but that doesn't mean she loves you less, or doesn't want you here. She's just trying to adjust. Change is uncommon in Woundabout."

The children nodded—the town seemed very stuck in its ways.

"Hey, if you're answering questions," Cordelia said, "do you know what the thing missing from the Mayor's house is?"

"There's something missing from the Mayor's

house?" Gray asked. Suddenly his face looked very not-neutral. His eyes lit up with excitement, and his lips curled into an expression the children thought was probably best described as "satisfied."

"Yeah," Cordelia said. "Something from a big glass box."

"Well," Gray said, standing, his face becoming neutral again, "I've never been in the Mayor's house since he moved in. So I'm not sure what he keeps in the glass box. But we'd better get going. I have to get to the store. Come on, I'll show you more of the town."

Chapter 8

When they left the park, Gray walked them through the town. They passed more houses, and also more businesses, including a post office that looked like a stamped letter from the front, and a pet shop that seemed to sell nothing but birds.

Along the way, everyone stopped and said hello to Gray. Gray lifted his hat to them. Many of them stared at the children, and some tried to look as if they weren't staring when they were.

Also along the way, the children kept their eyes out for the Mayor's missing thing. They had Kip

stand next to strange-looking lawn ornaments and mailboxes, to see if they were the right size. But nothing seemed to be special enough—and it was all out in public. If they were going to find the thing, it would be somewhere off the main streets, somewhere hidden.

Sometimes, Gray stopped and introduced the children to people. The people had different reactions. Mr. Phong, who was a barber, nodded at the children with a smile on his face. He wore an apron, and the giant barber's pole on his shop spun around and around like a peppermint stick. "It's good you're here," he said, though the children didn't know what he meant. Ms. Burbank, who was trimming the hedges in her garden with a pair of shears almost as large as her flowered

hat, looked down her pointed nose at Connor and Cordelia and made a harrumphing noise before turning away.

Mrs. Stein actually came running out of her furniture shop to say hello. She wore overalls and had her hair back in a ponytail. "It's so wonderful to meet you!" she said, bending down to shake each of their hands. "And what a cute dog!" she said, petting Kip's head. Connor started to correct her, but Mrs. Stein kept on talking. "We so seldom get new people, and never get new children. It's very exciting. It's like there's change again." She stood up and smiled hopefully at Gray when she said this, but he tilted his head slightly and stared at her until she nodded and went back into her shop, saying, "Nice to meet you, but I need to finish making this rocking chair!"

The children felt almost like celebrities. People seemed excited to see them or didn't want to have anything to do with them.

"Is it really so odd for new people to move into town?" Connor asked.

"Not so odd," Gray said. "But children are

unusual. The Mayor has rules, you know, about children. You're an exception."

"There are no children allowed in the town?" Cordelia asked.

"Not for extended periods," Gray said. "There are . . ." He paused, and stopped walking and scratched his chin. "There are conditions in the town that make it unhealthy for children to stay here too long. At least, according to the Mayor. So, for their own health, most children attend boarding school during the year, and then summer camp during the summer. That's where most of them are right now. Though there aren't many children here even when they are allowed back, for holidays and the like."

"So it's unhealthy for us to be here?" Connor asked. "Is it pollution?"

"No, no," Gray said, "nothing like that. You don't have to worry. It's only a month until school starts, and then you'll go away."

"We have to go to boarding school?" Cordelia asked, shocked to the point where her eyes felt wet. She was just getting used to their new home, and soon they'd have to leave again.

"Yes," Gray said. "Unless things have changed by then."

"Changed how?" Connor asked. "Environmental cleanup?"

"Something like that," Gray said. "But you shouldn't worry. Marigold will visit you every weekend, I'm sure of it. And I will, too." He stopped walking and knelt down to look the children in the eye. "I know, it's a new place, your life is different, and now you're finding out it will change again at the end of summer. But I promise, whatever your life here is going to be like, your aunt loves you very much and she's going to make that life the best she can. Okay?" The children nodded in unison. They believed him, but they were also scared about going away to another new place. "Plus, there will be children your age there."

"Can we bring Kip?" Connor asked.

"I believe they allow pets, yes," Gray said, standing. "And besides, maybe things will be different by then."

They walked along the street in silence for a few blocks more, Connor and Cordelia trying to picture boarding school. At least, they thought, they'd have each other, and silently reached out to hold hands.

When Gray stopped walking, they looked up to find themselves in front of a large supermarket with glass sliding doors that opened when they sensed him. A large sign over the doors said GRETEL'S GROCERY.

"Now, if you children see something you want to get for home, just let me know. Maybe a few treats—but not too many."

They went into the supermarket, which was even bigger than it looked from the outside. Brightly colored cans of vegetables and fruit made archways into each of the long aisles. Gray grabbed a shopping cart from the side of the store and took a list out of his pocket.

"We're not eating soup again, are we?" Cordelia asked as they followed Gray down the rows of food. There were brands and foods the children had

never seen before, almost all of them canned or frozen, in colors so bright they looked like toys rather than food.

"No." Gray smiled. "No more soup. I thought spaghetti and meatballs was probably a safe choice."

"Or broccoli," Cordelia said. She loved broccoli.

"Okay," Gray said, leading them over to a wall lined with vegetables and marked GREENHOUSE

FRESH! PICKED TODAY! "Broccoli it is." He chose two giant heads of broccoli and put them in the cart. They explored the rest of the grocery, going down aisle after aisle of huge boxes. The children checked the small back alleys of food, looking for something that didn't belong—the thing—but found nothing but food. Sometimes the children saw something that reminded them of home, but wasn't quite the same, like the Honey *Bits* cereal that looked like the Honey *Bites* cereal they were used to. Even the bear on the box looked almost the same, except this one wore a red shirt instead of a blue one. They stared at the box for a while before putting it in the cart. It wasn't quite the same as home and it felt wrong. Cordelia would have said it was like a blurry photo of her house, and Connor would have said it was like a house with the same outline but a different design. But they knew they were feeling the same thing. Before they bought their groceries, the children took the Honey Bits box out of the cart and ran to the cereal aisle to put it back. They took a cereal that was entirely unfamiliar to them, Grain Gears, instead.

When they had finished shopping and had all their groceries, the children and Gray set out again, the children keeping their eyes peeled for the Mayor's mysterious artifact.

Chapter 9

Outside, the sky was silvery and the wind was blowing stronger and colder than it had been before. The children rubbed their shoulders to keep warm. The walk to Aunt Marigold's house was mostly downhill, and sometimes Kip would notice a stone or a piece of trash that was blown just enough by the wind to start rolling downhill, and would chase after it. The children called him back each time, but he led them off track more than once. Luckily, Gray didn't seem to mind. He was smiling through it all. Once, Kip ran quite far ahead of them and Cordelia ran after him, yelling, "Come back here, Kip! Come back here right now!" Eventually she caught up to him and grabbed him by the leash—pretty hard, Connor thought. But she led him back to them, and everything seemed to be fine.

They walked by more houses and a few of the construction sites they'd seen when they came into town. But what was strange was that they were empty, the buildings still only half built. The children had thought before that they were closed because of the rain, but there was no rain now.

"Shouldn't there be people working there?" Connor asked, pointing at what looked like the skeleton of a tower, all metal rods—a frame for where the building would go. Down by the bottom, there were the beginnings of a brick wall, but it stopped one flight up.

"All construction was halted when the Mayor was elected," Gray said. "No new buildings."

"What?" Connor said. "That's ridiculous. Cities need new buildings to grow."

"The Mayor doesn't want the city to grow," Gray said. They were nearly at Aunt Marigold's house now.

"Why not?" Connor asked. "Couldn't new buildings make room for the people who want to move in? And they could bring in new jobs, and new stores and new ideas, which would bring in more people. A city with room to grow is a city with room to get better."

"I agree," Gray said in a soft voice. "But I'm not the Mayor."

They could see Aunt Marigold's house now, but Kip could see something else: a small pebble that was just starting to roll downhill. Off he went, chasing after it so fast that he yanked the leash from Cordelia's hand.

"Stupid!" Cordelia yelled. Connor stared at his sister for a moment. She'd never called Kip a name before. Kip seemed to understand that it wasn't normal, either, because he stopped and turned around, his head so low he was practically about to turn into a ball and roll away himself.

Connor ran forward and grabbed Kip's leash, and walked him back to Cordelia.

"I'd better start on dinner," Gray said, and walked toward the house. While Gray went inside,

Connor and Cordelia stopped outside. Connor took Kip off his leash and let him explore the front yard.

"Are you mad at Kip?" Connor asked Cordelia. Cordelia crossed her arms.

"No," she said. They sat down on the stairs leading up to Aunt Marigold's door.

"Do you think we'll like boarding school?" Connor asked.

"Maybe," Cordelia said. "I'm just sick of everything changing. I know Dad and Pop can't come back, but I wish we could at least be somewhere to stay." She kicked at the ground in front of her.

"Maybe we will stay here," Connor said. "Gray said if they finished the environmental cleanup, we could stay. And it's not so bad here. Kind of weird. But Aunt Marigold is nice, and Gray is nice."

"There are no other kids, though," Cordelia said. Back home, they had a few friends from neighboring farms whom they'd play with. "Maybe Nico, but he said he lives outside of town, and has to help his family work when he's in town, so he might not have time to hang out. Plus, I'm not sure he liked us very much."

"But there could be kids, if we're allowed to stay," Connor said. "And if we go to boarding school, there will be lots of other kids."

"Yeah," Cordelia said. She kicked at the ground again and leaned forward, putting her chin in her hands. "I'm not mad at Kip," she said. "Except when I am."

"When are you mad at him?" Connor asked slowly. Cordelia didn't look at him or answer for a long time, and the only sound was the wind.

"When I'm angry at Dad and Pop," Cordelia admitted. She felt so guilty saying it, but it was true. "When I'm mad at them for not testing the bomb's safety wire beforehand. And then sometimes I get mad at the capybaras who were supposed to find it faster . . . and then I get mad at all the capybaras, including Kip."

Connor took a deep breath. "I get mad at them, too," he said. "At night, I stare up at the ceiling and I get so angry that they even thought to use a real bomb, or even that they raised capybaras to sniff for bombs instead of raising something normal, like cows."

"You do?" Cordelia asked, looking up. Her eyes were watery, as if she was about to cry.

"Yeah," Connor said. "But really I think I'm just mad that they left. Even if it wasn't their fault." He put his arm around his sister and she leaned on his shoulder.

"Me too," Cordelia said. "I'm so angry that they left. And it's scary being here without them."

"Yeah," Connor said. "But you shouldn't yell at Kip."

"I'll try," Cordelia said, sniffling. Neither had known beforehand how angry the other one was, but knowing they weren't alone in feeling angry made them feel better, and less angry. It wasn't really their parents' fault, they knew, but being angry felt like one of the few things they could do besides being sad. Kip put his head on Cordelia's lap, and Cordelia reached down and stroked him. "I'm sorry, Kip," she said. "I know it's not your fault." Kip sighed contentedly and closed his eyes as Cordelia continued to pet him.

"What do you think Aunt Marigold is going to call Kip next?" Cordelia asked. "Maybe a ploppy panda?"

"A sloppy burro," Connor said, smiling.

"A nappy furball," Cordelia said, and the children giggled.

The door opened and the children looked up to see Aunt Marigold standing over them. She had a gold shawl wrapped around her, and it was so huge it looked like a mystical robe. They immediately stopped giggling, wondering if she'd heard them making fun of her.

"You're going to catch a cold out here," she said. "Come in for dinner." The children stood and followed her inside. "Also I found old photos of your dad and me growing up, if you want to look at them after dinner," she continued. "I mean, if you don't think it'll be upsetting."

"No, I think that would be nice," Cordelia said. Connor nodded.

"Good," Aunt Marigold said, and smiled. "Now, go bring in your chatty ferret and wash up for dinner."

"Okay," the children said, not correcting her, and trying very hard not to laugh.

Chapter 10

Dinner was delicious. Gray and Aunt Marigold had cooked it together, but the children guessed that Gray had been in charge because Aunt Marigold seemed to be constantly surprised by the meal: "Why, these are red pepper flakes!" "I think there's vegetable broth in this!" "This broccoli is steamed!"

When the meal was finished, as she had promised, Aunt Marigold took the children into the living room, where they sat on either side of her on a big green sofa and looked at the photos in the album on her lap. It was weird seeing their dad at their age. Connor would have said it was like X-ray vision you couldn't turn off—seeing through buildings to the beams and metal holding them up; Cordelia would have said it was like uploading your photos to your computer and finding a whole group of pictures you didn't take. But they both knew it was the same thing.

"That's your dad's eighth birthday," Aunt Marigold said, pointing at a photo of a little boy wearing a party hat in front of a cake shaped like a giant mouse. "Oh, and here's his high school

graduation." They could tell Aunt Marigold felt the same way they did (although they weren't sure how she would describe it, maybe like driving your first car again, decades later).

Her voice shook a little, and her eyes were wet.

"Do you know what camera these were taken with?" Cordelia asked, as a way of distracting their aunt from her unhappiness.

Aunt Marigold laughed. "Oh, an old one, I'd imagine," she said, wiping away

a tear that could have been from the laugh, or from

something else. "I'm sorry, I don't know much about cameras."

"It looks like a Polaroid SX-Seventy," Cordelia said. "Like mine!" She held up her camera. It had been her dad's, and his dad's before that, even if the insides were new.

"Actually," Aunt Marigold said, looking at the camera, "it could be that one. Your dad loved it. I was never good with a camera."

"Maybe there's a camera shop in town?" Connor asked. "I bet Cordelia could show you how to take photos."

"That would be fun!" Cordelia said.

"That would be fun," Aunt Marigold said, and smiled. "But I don't think there is one. Maybe Gray can take you to the next town over."

"No," Cordelia said. "I want you to come, too." She took Aunt Marigold's hand, and Aunt Marigold looked down and took a sudden, deep breath.

"Are you okay?" Connor asked.

"Oh, yes," Aunt Marigold said. She reached out with her other hand and looked as though she was going to take Connor's, but then she pulled her hand back, as if she was scared. But then she stuck her chin out, and as if she were heading for a finish line, she took Connor's hand and clasped it, warmly. She was holding their hands in her own, and she pulled them to her chest and turned to look at each of them. "I'm so happy you're here," she said.

The children thought this was all rather odd, but they knew she was missing her brother, just as they were missing their parents, and people do strange things when they grieve. They also knew she loved them.

"But there must be a camera store in town," Cordelia said. "All those photos at the Mayor's house had to be professionally developed."

"Oh," Aunt Marigold said, dropping their hands and looking back down at the photo album, "those were from his life before."

"Before?" Connor asked. He knew it was a question, but Aunt Marigold only seemed to mind questions when the Mayor was nearby.

"He and his sister, Nadia, used to travel the

world," Aunt Marigold said. "Explore ruins and shipwrecks and jungles. Or so I've heard."

"Nadia must be the one who took the photos," Cordelia said. "She'll know where the camera store is. Can we call her?"

"Oh, Nadia doesn't live in Woundabout," Aunt Marigold said. She closed the photo album and stood up from the sofa. "She still travels the world, exploring old castles, underground cities. . . ."

"Without her brother?" Connor asked.

"Ah, well," Aunt Marigold said, putting the photo album on the shelf, "the Mayor is a bit sick, you see. He can't travel like he used to."

"He didn't look sick," Cordelia said. Kip clambered up onto the sofa where Aunt Marigold had been sitting and laid his head in Cordelia's lap.

"It's the air in Woundabout," Aunt Marigold said, turning around. "It's good for him. Oh, your lappy boar took my seat."

"He's a capybara." Connor laughed. "He can get down if you want."

"Why don't we all cram on together and watch a

movie?" Aunt Marigold said. "One of my favorites
has a photojournalist I think you'll like, Cordelia."

"Okay," the children said, and they pushed Kip
around so that he wasn't taking up much space and
Aunt Marigold could sit back down. Gray, apparently knowing what they were doing, came in with
popcorn, and they watched the movie, which took
place in the early 1900s and had lots of good stuff,
such as a photojournalist, car races, and a really
big pie fight. They ate popcorn and watched the
movie, and when it was over, Aunt Marigold kissed

them each on the forehead (even Kip) and told them to go change into their pajamas. After they changed and brushed their teeth, though, and Aunt Marigold was tucking them in, Cordelia looked up at her and said, "I'm sorry about your boyfriend." Aunt Marigold dropped the sheet and took a step backward, and Cordelia sat up, afraid she'd done something wrong.

"I'm sorry," Cordelia said. "Gray told us. He said it was sad we didn't know much about you."

"Oh," Aunt Marigold said, sitting on the bed. "I guess that's true. And thank you. It was a long, long time ago. Benny was a good man, though." She looked down at her hands, which were clutched together like a knotted ball of yarn. "But let's not talk about that." She stood up and tucked Cordelia in, and then tucked Connor in, and kissed them both on the forehead again and wished them good night.

It rained again in the night, waking the children up. Heavy sheets of water poured down their windows, making the glass look like melted sugar, and thunder and lightning roared like a marching band on the roof. Cordelia went into Connor's

room and together they stared out the window in their pajamas.

"The Mayor's sister left him all alone when he got sick," Connor said, staring at the rain.

"She sends him postcards, though," Cordelia said. "Remember all the postcards?"

"Yeah, but it's not the same," Connor said, sitting down on the bed. "If we explored the world together, and I got sick, would you go on without me?"

"No!" Cordelia said, sitting down next to him.

"Of course not. You're my brother, and I wouldn't leave you. I'd stay with you until you got better." She leaned her head on his shoulder. "But I do hope we can travel the world someday, and have exciting adventures."

"Me too," Connor said. "And that's what I'd do for you, too. I'd stay until you were better. It makes me feel sad for the Mayor."

"Yeah," Cordelia said. They reached out and held each other's hands, thinking of the abandoned Mayor, alone in his windy house full of postcards.

"Maybe the thing," Cordelia said, "is something that reminds him of his sister. Something they found together."

"But then why would the rest of the town care about it?" Connor asked. Cordelia shrugged. They still didn't know what the Mayor's missing thing was. They knew it wasn't too heavy, and not bigger than Kip, and that it wasn't in the grocery. They knew it was dangerous, but not why. They thought maybe it had something to do with the strange things in the town—the air, the matches, maybe even why no questions were allowed—but they weren't sure.

It hadn't been a very productive day. They both sighed, realizing this, and Cordelia frowned.

"We'll look some more tomorrow," Connor said. "Maybe we can sneak out of the park and explore the rest of town."

"Maybe," Cordelia said. They both closed their eyes and tried to imagine what the thing was as they fell asleep.

Chapter 11

The next morning, Gray made them pancakes for breakfast. While they ate, Aunt Marigold told them she was going to look through the garage for some more old photos, and call some of the neighbors to ask about a camera shop.

"We can help with that," Cordelia offered, but Aunt Marigold shook her head.

"No, no," she said.

"You need to go to the park with Gray again. Stick to your routine. Someone might notice if you don't."

"I wonder if that would be bad," Connor said, struggling to ask a question without a question mark.

Aunt Marigold stood up and put her dishes in the sink. "It's so nice out today," she said. "Of course you should go to the park." The children looked out the window. It did look like a nice day. They shrugged, and after they'd bathed and dressed, they headed out with Gray for the park. They passed many of the same people from yesterday, who waved, or sometimes didn't. Kip pulled

tight on his leash, knowing where they were headed this time, and Cordelia giggled at how excited he was.

When they finally got to the park, Gray sat down with his paper as he had yesterday, and the children took out some toys for Kip. But before they could even start tossing the Frisbee around, they heard a voice behind them.

"What is that thing, anyway?"

They turned around. It was Nico, the boy from yesterday.

"He's a capybara," Connor said. "Like a giant guinea pig."

Nico walked over and cautiously patted Kip on the head. "Cute," he said. "Weird, but cute."

"I thought you didn't like the park when it was crowded," Cordelia said in an accusing voice.

"Yeah," Nico said. "Sorry. I was a bit rude, wasn't I? I didn't mean to be. I was just jealous. You lot moving in and all while my sister and folks and I still have to live outside."

"That's not our fault, though," Cordelia said.

"I know," Nico said.

"I'm sorry the Mayor won't let you move in," Cordelia said.

"Me too," Connor said. "The Mayor didn't seem very nice when we met him."

"He ain't," Nico said. "We want to move in 'cause my sister—she had this accident. And since then, she doesn't leave her lab ever. We used to go out and play every day, and we'd make these race cars and drive them around . . . but now she's just inside all day. I think, if we got to move into town, things might go back to how they were." Connor and Cordelia nodded in sympathy. They knew what it was like to want things to go back to the way they were.

"Is there anything we can do?" Cordelia asked.

"Yeah," Connor said. "Maybe your sister can stay with our aunt for a while? I don't know how the air here works—Gray said it's bad for kids—but if it'll just take a week, I bet no one would notice."

Nico smiled. "That's real gallant of you," he said. "I don't know how it works, either. I don't even know what the air is supposed to do, exactly. Not sure my folks do, either. But I think we need to live here. Which we need the Mayor's permission for. But . . ." He stopped talking and walked over to one of the bare trees, and motioned them to follow. The children did, so they were all in a huddle, and Nico continued in a soft voice. "Can you keep a secret?" he asked. Connor and Cordelia nodded. "I have a plan. But you have to help me look for something."

"Like hide-and-seek?" Cordelia asked.

"Nah, like hidden treasure!" Nico said. "There's this thing . . . you'll know it if you see it. I hid it . . . buried it here. But now I can't find it."

"What is it?" Cordelia asked, wondering if it could be the Mayor's thing that they were looking for.

"It's like a pipe," Nico said. "Like I said, you'll know it when you see it."

"Where did you get it?" Connor asked. If it was a piece of broken pipe from somewhere, it meant that a water line or sewage line or some other kind of important line could be damaged.

Nico narrowed his eyes and looked over to where Gray was sitting, reading his newspaper.

"Come with me," he said, walking even farther away from Gray and into a clump of trees, the children following. "You have to promise not to tell."

Connor and Cordelia looked at each other, then looked back at Nico and nodded.

"I stole it," Nico said proudly.

Chapter 12

W hat?" Cordelia said loudly. Nico put a finger to her lips to quiet her. Cordelia wiped her mouth. "Ew," she said. "Shhhh," he said. "You promised not to tell."

"But why would you steal it?" Connor asked. "Is it an important pipe? Did you steal it from the Mayor?"

"Yeah." Nico shrugged. "Stole it from the Mayor. But it's not really a pipe. . . . And I nick stuff all the time. I practice. I'm good with my hands."

"So you stole it just to steal it?" Cordelia asked, her eyes growing wide. She knew stealing was bad, but Nico seemed so proud of it that she thought maybe it was impressive, too.

"Well . . . no," Nico confessed. "Not this one. This one I stole 'cause it's important to the Mayor. And I thought if I stole it, I could promise to give it back . . . if he let my family move into town. Then my sister might be better and we could . . ." Nico looked away for a moment. "If we move here, things will be good again."

"Do you know why it's important to the Mayor?" Cordelia asked. She felt as if they were closer to unraveling the mystery of the thing—the pipe—and maybe that might explain some of the weirdness of the town.

Nico shrugged. "Dunno. But it is. He keeps it in a fancy case, so yesterday, when he was out talking to my dad about what vegetables the town needed, I slipped in through a window and opened the case and took it."

"He's been sending out search parties to look for it, you know," Cordelia said.

"Yeah," Nico said. "But I didn't want anyone to find it, so I buried it. . . ." He walked farther into the clump of trees. "I buried it here," he said, pointing to a place in the ground that had been dug up. "But it's gone. I think maybe the rain washed it away. So, want to help me look for it?"

Connor and Cordelia looked at each other, uneasy about helping a thief. But he'd stolen from the Mayor, and they didn't really like the Mayor, so it didn't seem as though he'd done anything *too* wrong. He was planning on giving it back, after all. And besides, if they found the thing—the pipe—maybe they'd understand why it was so important, and if it had to do with the rest of the town's strangeness.

"Okay," Connor said. "We can help." Connor whistled once and called out, "Kip!" A few moments later, a dripping-wet Kip came running up to them from the pond, shaking the muddy water off himself.

"What is that thing again?" Nico asked, looking as if he wanted to run away.

"A capybara," Cordelia said. "He's very friendly. Like a big guinea pig, with only slightly better table manners." Kip snorted. "He'll help."

"How?"

"You'll see."

"Kip," Connor said, "something's gone missing from here." Connor pointed at the place where Nico had buried the pipe, or whatever it was. Kip ran forward and sniffed around the spot for a while, his nostrils flexing and making little huffing noises. He raised his nose into the air and sniffed there, too. He started walking away from the spot. The three of them followed. He led them out of the clump of trees and down a hill. The park was all dirt, and the storm had left little dried riverbeds all over from the rain rushing downhill. He led them over to the side of the park, to the wall, and stopped there.

Nico ran forward to see where Kip was standing.

It was a hole in the wall, a pretty big one, large enough for a house cat. It was at ground level, and it looked as though it had just worn away over time.

"Blast it!" Nico shouted in frustration. "It could be anywhere. The rain could have taken it anywhere."

"We can search the town," Connor said. "I want to map it anyway."

"Yeah," Nico said. "That sounds all right."

"Nico!" called a voice. The three of them turned around. A tall man in a plaid shirt and suspenders was walking toward them.

"That's my dad. I'm going to have to go," Nico said, disappointed. "But if you find it, just bury it back in the spot. Maybe put rocks around it this time so it don't wash away."

"You haven't even told us what it is," Connor said. Nico opened his mouth to say something, but then his father was standing over them.

"Hello, Nico," his dad said.

"Hi, Dad," Nico said. "This is Connor and

Cordelia. They're the new kids. They moved here 'cause their parents died. So I guess the Mayor made an exception for them."

"I guess so," Nico's dad said. He smiled down at the children, but it was a tight smile, the kind you force yourself to make when you're being told to smile and don't want to. "Nice to meet you. C'mon, Nico, we have to get back to the greenhouses. There's a whole crop of cucumbers to pack up."

"Yeah, okay. Bye, Connor, Cordelia. Maybe I'll see you tomorrow?" Nico said.

"I think we'll be here," Connor said. "It's our routine . . . or something."

"Spiffy," Nico said. "So I know where to find you. Bye, then." Nico waved once at them, then he and his father walked out of the park. Nico's father didn't even stop to talk to Gray.

"So, you want to look for this thing?" Connor asked his sister.

"I don't know how we'll get out of the park, though," Cordelia said. "And Aunt Marigold didn't want us wandering."

The children walked back toward the center of the park, and Kip followed after them. They lay down in the grass and stared up at the sky. Though the park was beige and colorless, the sky seemed to be the brightest blue they'd ever seen.

"I wish we were home," Cordelia said.

"Me too." They stared at the sky for a while longer, maybe hoping they'd wake up from a very odd dream. But they didn't.

"Let's play Frisbee with Kip," Cordelia said. Playing with Kip always made them happy. They

used to take him out every day after school and toss the Frisbee with him, when they lived on the ranch. When their parents were done with their work for the day, they would come and join the game, all four of them tossing the Frisbee back and forth while Kip tried to leap up and grab it.

Connor got out the Frisbee and tossed it, and Kip ran after it, jumping into the air to catch it in his mouth. His two large teeth clamped shut on it, and he ran over to Cordelia, who took the Frisbee from him and threw it again. They threw it back and forth for a while, Kip running to catch it. Suddenly, Connor's eyes lit up and he smiled.

"I have an idea," he said, and threw the Frisbee again, this time too far and on its side, so that Kip couldn't catch it. It landed still on its side, like the wheel of a car. The park, like the whole town, was on a hill, so the Frisbee started to roll downhill. Kip looked around to see where it was, but it was already rolling out of the park gate and down through town. Kip took off after it.

"Kip!" Cordelia called, but it was too late. Kip was running downhill and out of the park. The children looked at each other and ran out of the park after him.

"Children!" Gray called out, and with a sigh, got up and chased after them, too.

Chapter 13

They all ran downhill. First the Frisbee, which wasn't running, but rolling. Then came Kip, chasing the Frisbee. Then came Cordelia and Connor, chasing Kip. And finally came Gray, chasing the children while holding his hat on his head so it didn't fly away.

The Frisbee seemed to know the streets of the town, because it turned with them and rolled through lawns and over bridges and never fell over. It just kept rolling downhill. When it finally stopped, the children were just behind it. They were at the bottom of the hill, far from any houses.

They couldn't see anyone else around them, and the world felt empty. The grass here was much taller and a brighter green than the grass in the park. The Frisbee rolled around in a circle a few times and fell over, as if all that rolling had tired it out.

Kip leapt on the Frisbee, picked it up with his large teeth, and brought it over to Connor, who was bent over, trying to catch his breath from the long run.

"Good boy," Connor managed to say between pants.

"Where are we?" Cordelia asked, taking out her camera.

"Just outside town," said Gray, catching up to them. "We should get back."

"It's prettier here," Cordelia said, taking photos with her camera. She took one of the town, which looked peaceful so far away and with the blue sky behind it. She took some of the grass, too. Suddenly, Kip dropped the Frisbee and began sniffing the air. He turned back toward the town and started running again.

"Kip!" Connor shouted. "Come back! We're tired!" But Kip kept running, and the children were forced to chase after him some more. He stopped near the edge of town, where there was especially tall grass, and he began sniffing it again. The children followed him into the grass, which was nearly as tall as they were, pushing it aside like window curtains. They saw something glint in the grass and walked toward it.

"What's that?" Cordelia asked.

Lying in the grass was a large handle, like the kind on the side of a jack-in-the-box. Kip was sniffing it, but when he saw Connor and Cordelia, he looked up at them, seeming pleased with himself.

"It's a crank," Connor said, picking it up. It was half as big as Kip. "A big crank."

"Do you think this is what Nico was talking about? What he stole?"

"Maybe. . . . Kip did have its scent, and it is sort of like a pipe. But why would the Mayor find a crank so valuable?"

"Maybe he found it on one of his adventures," Cordelia said, "and it's a sacred treasure from a ruined city."

The children looked it over. Cordelia took it from Connor. It wasn't as heavy as it looked, but it was solid. The handle was wood, and the rest of it was metal. On the end without the handle, it had an eight-sided pole sticking from it. There were no jewels on it, though, and it didn't seem to be made of gold or silver. It was just a crank.

"I think this would fit in the holes," Connor said. "The ones we found in the park."

"We should try it," Cordelia said. Her eyes grew wide as she wondered what a crank and a hole in the grass could do. If nothing else, it would make an interesting photo.

Gray came up behind them. He stared down at the crank Connor held, and his eyebrows rose, but he said nothing.

"We just found it," Connor said, not wanting to get Nico in trouble. "Do you know what it does?"

"We should get home," Gray said, looking at the sky. "I still need to buy groceries, and your aunt has dinner every night at seven."

"Part of her routine?" Cordelia asked. She sounded angrier than she meant to.

"Yes," Gray said. "Routine is important in this town. Even if you don't have one, it is best to appear as though you do." His expression was entirely neutral as he said this.

"What time do you get home?" Cordelia asked, coming up with an idea.

"Five o'clock sharp." Gray looked at his watch. "It is three now."

"So you're going to go to the store," Connor said, "and be home exactly at five. If we went somewhere else—"

"Like the park," Cordelia said.

"But arrived home exactly at five, it would

137

seem as though we were arriving home *with* you," Connor finished.

"It might seem that way, yes," Gray said. "I'm going to head to the store now. I hope you children follow closely and don't get lost and wind up somewhere else." He turned around and walked back into town. The children smiled at each other and headed back to the park.

Chapter 14

Connor remembered the way they had come, and he led them back as quickly as he could. He had a memory for streets and how they were interwoven, so it was easy for him to find the way. But the walk was uphill this time, not downhill, and that made it hard to go very fast. By the time the children reached the park, it was four o'clock, and they were very tired.

"We don't have much time," Cordelia said. She was holding the crank in her sweaty hands. "We can try winding it a few times, but then we have to head home if we want to make it in time."

"Okay," Connor said. "Let's do it."

Cordelia found the strange hole they'd looked at before in the park and fitted the crank into it. It fell into place with a little click that seemed to vibrate the dirt under their shoes.

"So now we wind it?" Cordelia asked. Connor nodded. Neither of them reached forward to take it. "What do you think will happen?" Cordelia asked.

"Well," Connor said, thinking about parks and their purpose in towns and cities as displays of nature and places to play and relax, "Capability Brown, one of the first park designers, would say that the ideal park is about views, and creating a poem with nature. Maybe the crank will start the fountain up, or raise some poles with flags, so the view is nicer." He took a step away from the crank and looked out over the park's vista. It was flat and brown. There were no views, no layers. "Or, Calvert Vaux, one of the designers of Central Park, in New York, might say a park needs an 'irregular, discon- nected featureless conglomeration of ground.'"

"Huh?" said Cordelia.

"It needs to be random—like nature. So maybe," Connor said, sweeping his hands out over the ground, "it shoots lots of seeds into the air from tiny holes in the ground, and it waters them. Then, over time, a new park grows over this one—all based on where the seeds happen to land. Random like nature."

"That would be nice," Cordelia said, dragging a line through the dirt with her shoe, "but it would take a long time."

"Yeah," Connor said. "But maybe the fountain will at least go on." He turned back to the crank, and they stepped forward and both put their hands on it.

"We'll wind it together," Cordelia said. "On three. Ready?" She knew it was just a weird old crank, but it felt very exciting.

"Yeah," Connor said.

"One . . . two . . . three!" They began winding. It was a little hard to wind at first, like pushing a large stone uphill, but then it became easier and they were winding and winding. There was a sound like someone very small letting out a very large breath he'd been holding forever. But nothing else. They kept winding.

Suddenly, the dead, empty trees around them began to shake. The children wound the crank more. It was going faster now, as though it had become slippery and was easier to wind. The branches of the trees seemed to creak upward and grow, their dark limbs lightening, the tips stretching like chewed gum. Small bumps appeared on the tree branches. And as the children wound, those bumps grew and opened up into giant lavender flowers and small green leaves. The dirt under their feet suddenly sprang up with grass. The flowers on the trees, all as large as basketballs, practically exploded, sending petals down around the children's heads like snow. And finally, the fountain burst to life, shooting water high into the air and causing ripples in the pond.

The park was alive now. And beautiful. It was the most beautiful thing either of the children had ever seen. The trees were tall and green and blooming lavender. The grass smelled fresh and mingled with the perfume of the fallen petals. They could

hear crickets somewhere, and the soft hum of insects coming out just before sunset. Kip ran around the park, snorting and sniffing at the flowers and grass, trying to explore the new park as quickly as possible. Connor and Cordelia stared at it in wonder. It was as if they could breathe again, somehow. Connor picked a petal out of his hair and stared at its texture of small lines. He pressed it to his face. It was soft and cool. Cordelia took photo after photo, wanting to make the moment last forever.

"How?" Cordelia finally asked. She didn't even know what question she meant, but she knew Connor would understand.

"I don't know," he said. "Maybe it's a machine. Like in a museum diorama to show how plants grow."

"But these are real," Cordelia said, picking up a flower petal and smelling it. "These are real flowers. At the museum they're made of plastic. Can a machine make flowers bloom?"

"I didn't think so," Connor said. "I've never heard of it."

"Maybe it's magic," Cordelia said.

Connor usually would have said he didn't think magic was real, but staring at the park, he thought that even if it wasn't magic that made it grow, it sure looked and felt like magic.

"If it's magic, that would explain why the Mayor wanted it," added Cordelia.

"But if the Mayor had it for so long, why would he have kept the park like it was before?"

"'Cause he's a mean old crank," Cordelia said, and smiled a little at her pun. "The crank kept the crank."

"We should let Nico know we found it, too."

"You mean bury it, where he asked us to?" Cordelia asked. She didn't want to give up the crank. It was powerful and she wanted to keep it with them. She wanted to make sure it was safe. Connor felt the same way.

"Maybe we can just leave a note," Connor said. "To let him know we found it, and what it did, and that we're holding on to it so it doesn't wash away."

"That sounds good," Cordelia said. So they used the paper and pencil Connor had brought and wrote out a note explaining everything, and put it where Nico had buried the crank originally, held in place by a stone.

"We have to get home," Connor said with a sigh. "We're going to be late."

"I know," Cordelia said. "We can come back tomorrow, right?"

"Yeah," Connor said. They stared at the park a little longer.

Connor pulled the crank out of the socket. It clicked as it came out, but the trees stayed blooming, and the fountain continued to spray. They had wound up the park, and it looked as though it would stay this way for a while.

Cordelia put the crank in her bag, where it bulged suspiciously, and they hurried home. No one stopped them; no one looked at them. They got home at four fifty-nine and saw Gray standing in the front yard, holding bags of groceries. He nodded at them, then opened the door and walked in, as though they'd been with him the entire time.

"Gray? Children?" came the sound of Aunt Marigold's voice.

"Hi, Aunt Marigold," Connor called.

"Did you have a nice day?" came her voice again. Cordelia looked around for somewhere to hide the crank.

"Yes," Cordelia called. "But we need to go wash up now. Then we'll tell you about it."

"That sounds lovely," Aunt Marigold called back. The children went upstairs as quickly as they could and hid the crank under Cordelia's bed. Then they washed up and went downstairs for dinner, both smiling with the strange, new secret they had discovered.

Chapter 15

id you have fun at the park?" Aunt Marigold asked over dinner that night. They were having a tasty stir-fry with asparagus and rice.

"It was sort of barren," Connor said, deciding it would be best not to tell anyone about the park yet.

"Yes, it's always been like that. No one really goes there."

"And we made friends with Nico," Cordelia said.

Aunt Marigold tilted her head like an owl. "I don't know any Nico."

"Mr. and Mrs. Calander's son," Gray said. "They run the greenhouses outside town."

"Oh. . . . Well, I don't know if you should really be talking too much with people from outside town . . . but I'm glad you enjoyed yourselves."

Cordelia and Connor nodded, but shared a look when Aunt Marigold turned away. They themselves were technically outsiders, weren't they?

After dinner, the children, Aunt Marigold, and Gray went to the den and watched a movie together. It was a funny movie with a leopard that people had to sing to, but Connor and Cordelia kept thinking about the crank, and the other places in town where they could wind it, and the other magical things that might happen. Aunt Marigold fell asleep on the sofa, and Gray put a blanket over her. Cordelia and Connor went back up to bed and closed themselves in Cordelia's room. They took the crank out from under the bed and stared at it. It was just a piece of metal, but somehow it had made trees bloom.

"I want to try it in the other holes we saw," Cordelia whispered.

"Me too," Connor whispered back. Neither of

149

them had ever been particularly bad children, but they'd never really felt as hemmed in as they did now. It was as if the weird streets of the town were a knot or spiderweb that they were caught in, and when they tried to move, it just got tighter.

"You think we should give it back to the Mayor?" Cordelia asked.

"I don't know," Connor said after a moment. "He made it sound dangerous—like a weapon. He didn't want it falling into the wrong hands, remember? But this is a good thing. It made the park bloom. Why would anyone want to stop that? Especially a Mayor, whose job is to make a town its best?"

"Yeah," Cordelia said. "The Mayor was mean, but I don't understand how anyone could hate a beautiful park. This crank is magic." She stroked the crank as though it were Kip. Kip jealously nudged his head under her hand so that she was petting him instead. "We should keep it. Just for now. Until we understand it better."

"We *could* sneak out," Connor said. "I made a map—I know part of the town. We can try it on those other holes."

If asked, the children would describe their desire to wind the crank in more holes very differently: Connor would describe it as the need to demolish a run-down building, so that a better one could be built in its place, and Cordelia would say it had been like the need to develop an old roll of film found in the corner of the closet. But they both knew it was the same thing.

"And we could look for more holes," Cordelia said. So the children pulled up their covers and pretended to sleep until they couldn't hear anyone walking around in the house. They took the crank out from under the bed and grabbed some flashlights they'd found in an upstairs closet. Kip followed them out of the room. They walked quietly down the stairs. The lights were out in the main entryway, so they used their flashlights to find the door. They opened it very quietly and closed it behind them. They didn't make a noise until they were four houses away.

No one seemed to be awake. The town was completely dark, and only their flashlights and Connor's map, though it was unfinished and small,

kept them from feeling completely lost. Even Kip seemed nervous, staying close to their legs and not running out of the range of the flashlights.

"Let's go to the statue first," Connor said, looking at his map.

He directed them there, flashlight in hand. They passed by Mrs. Washburn's laundry, which blew in the breeze like ghosts, and they passed a bakery they hadn't noticed before, with a big sign in the shape of a loaf of bread that said PAIN on it. Connor knew it was the French word for "bread" and whispered it to his sister, but it still seemed spooky, blowing back and forth in the wind. They passed a few more stores, the hat shop, and an old building with a carving of a windmill over the door before they came to the statue.

The woman still held her hands out, as if begging. Connor went around the statue and stuck the

153

crank into her back; Cordelia took a photo before they started winding, to compare afterward. Then, together, they wound the crank.

"What's she doing?" Connor asked, looking up as they wound.

"She's moving," Cordelia said. They heard a click and the crank wouldn't wind anymore, so they pulled it out and went around to look at her, comparing her with the photo Cordelia had taken beforehand. The woman's head had moved, so it seemed she was looking right at them, and the corners of her mouth were raised slightly. Her hands began to move. The movements weren't natural or fluid, but jerky, like a puppet's. She straightened up and uncoiled her legs, so she wasn't kneeling on the podium but sitting on it like a chair. She kept moving her hands, holding one hand up, palm flat, fingers extended. She closed all her fingers but one, as though she were counting. The other hand rose up and pointed at the river.

"What is she pointing at?" Cordelia asked, taking a photo. Connor looked down at his map.

"I think she's pointing at the hole by the river."

"She's pointing at another place for the crank?" Cordelia asked.

Connor shrugged. "That's what it looks like from my map," he said. "We should go over there anyway, to check it out."

Taking the crank, the children walked quietly to the river and over the bridge. The water looked inky black in the darkness. It was so still it barely broke the silence of the night.

"What do you think will happen here?" Cordelia asked.

"I have no idea," Connor said. "I didn't think a crank could make grass grow and flowers bloom."

"Maybe fish will jump out of the water. Or the water will turn gold," Cordelia said, taking a photo

of the river. The flash from her camera reflected off the still water like a mirror, and for a moment, the whole city felt lit up. Connor and Cordelia became very quiet, hoping no one had seen them.

There was no sound except the soft murmur of the slow-moving river, like a dripping faucet.

"Okay," Connor said, and stuck the crank into the hole in the ground by the river. He started to turn it. This one was harder to push. It felt not stuck exactly, but heavy, as though whatever he was cranking weighed hundreds and hundreds of pounds. And nothing seemed to happen as he cranked. He wound the crank around three times and then he had to stop to catch his breath. Cordelia was still looking around, trying to find whatever was changing.

"Wait, do you hear that?" she asked. Connor shook his head. All he could hear was his own panting.

Cordelia looked over the edge, at the river. The water was moving now. Slowly, like a brook, but steadily. It made the sound of a faucet dribbling water, instead of just dripping it.

"The river is flowing," she said, and took a photo, the flash lighting up the town again for a moment,

like lightning. "Crank it again." Connor stood and started pushing and this time Cordelia helped him, and they wound it five more times. When they stopped, they could hear the river rushing before they even looked over the edge. It was moving fast, and pushing against the brick walls on either side, white foam lashing up and spraying their faces like rain.

"Wow," Cordelia said, taking a photo. They stared at the water for a few minutes, enjoying the cool spray on their faces. The water made them feel relaxed somehow, like a day at the beach. "Let's go back and see the statue. If she was pointing at this crank-hole, maybe she's pointing somewhere else now."

The children walked back over the bridge. They were faster now, and louder, excited by the sound of moving water and the sense that the town was more alive than it had been before.

The statue had changed. Now she held up two fingers on one hand, and pointed in another direction.

"Where does that one point?" Cordelia asked, taking another photo.

"I don't know. It's almost like she's pointing *into* the cliff." The statue was pointing in the direction of the rising slope of the city, but instead of pointing up along it, she seemed to be just jabbing her finger at it. "Do you want to see if there's a door, or maybe a building she's pointing at? Go a little farther on?"

Cordelia looked down at Kip, who was nervously pressing himself against her leg.

"I think . . ." Cordelia said. "Maybe that's enough for the night. I don't want to get in trouble if someone realizes we're out of bed."

"Yeah," Connor said. "I was thinking the same thing. Plus, who knows what effect the river will have on the town? It could start up a water mill, or flood someplace. . . . It's better if we wait before we try anything else. Let's see what happens."

"You think we could have just accidentally flooded someone?" Cordelia asked, pulling at the hem of her skirt with worry. She imagined people's houses filling with water and people floating away on beds in the middle of the night.

"Probably not . . ." Connor said. "The banks of the river have been walled over. But maybe we flooded a crop field somewhere. Like, a dry one, and it's growing now, just like the park."

"That would be cool." Cordelia yawned.

"We can look for more tomorrow," Connor said, "when we're supposed to be at the park."

"*This* will be our routine," Cordelia said, and the children giggled.

Connor looked at his map. "Aunt Marigold's house is this way."

At home, the children opened the door very quietly and snuck back up the stairs to bed. There they put on their pajamas and hid the crank under Cordelia's bed again. They lay down on the blanket on the floor, Kip already asleep between them and snoring.

"I bet Dad and Pop would have thought all this cranking was really cool," Cordelia said into the darkness.

"They would have loved it," Connor said. He and Cordelia were quiet for a long time, but they each knew the other one was awake.

"I miss them," Connor said.

"Me too," Cordelia said.

Chapter 16

The next morning, the children ate breakfast in bed, washed and dressed, and went downstairs as though they hadn't been sneaking around town last night. Gray was at the sink when they went into the kitchen, and Aunt Marigold was reading a book at the table. Gray looked over at them in his usual neutral way.

"Did you sleep well?" he asked. The children nodded. "Good. I'm not quite ready to go yet. Let me make you some tea while I finish the washing."

They were drinking their tea with little biscuits when someone rang the doorbell. It rang once, and then over and over again very quickly before Gray could answer the door. The doorbell sounded frightened.

"No one comes over this early," Aunt Marigold said. She looked worried. She bunched her dressing gown around her and retied its belt very tightly.

Mrs. Washburn ran into the kitchen suddenly. She was holding a basket of wet laundry that she hadn't yet hung out to dry.

"Marigold!" she shouted, though Aunt Marigold was right there. "The river! It's . . . moving." She said the word *moving* in a whisper. The children looked at each other and then very quickly looked back at their tea. Gray went back into the kitchen.

"No," Aunt Marigold said. "That's impossible. The Mayor wouldn't allow it."

"Come see!" Mrs. Washburn said, and raced out of the room, leaving a trail of water where her wet laundry had dripped.

Aunt Marigold stared after her,

163

then dashed out of the room. A moment later she ran by the kitchen door, wearing a coat over her robe.

"What's so strange about the river moving?" Connor asked Gray in what he hoped was an innocent tone.

"It doesn't," Gray said without looking up.

"But all rivers move," Connor said.

"Yes, but ours moved as little as possible. Until now, it appears."

The children studied Gray, wondering if he knew that they were responsible. But he didn't look up, and they couldn't tell from his tone of voice.

"Maybe we should go look," Cordelia said. Connor nodded, and they got up and left the kitchen, dragging along Kip, who was trying to eat what was left of the biscuits off their plates.

Chapter 17

They gathered their things and headed outside to see the river. Even if they hadn't known where it was, it would have been easy to spot. People were lined up on either side of the river and over the bridge, all of them staring down at the rushing water.

"The sound is so soothing," the children heard someone say as they walked. They spotted Aunt Marigold and pushed themselves so that they were on either side of her, looking down at the river. She didn't even notice. She was staring at the water and mumbling very softly to herself.

"Ohdearohdearohdearohdearohdear."

"Is everything okay?" Connor asked. "It's just a river."

"It isn't supposed to be moving this quickly," Aunt Marigold said. "It means things are *changing*."

"Is that bad?" Cordelia asked.

"Of course it's bad," said the Mayor, appearing suddenly behind them. "We keep things steady here. As little change as we can. We may not be able to control the weather, but . . . everything else"— he swept his hand out in front of him, gesturing at the whole town—"we keep it from changing. When things change, it's bad. Your parents' death was a change. You're fond of questions, so let me ask you: did you enjoy that?"

"N-no," Connor stammered. Both the children suddenly felt ashamed of themselves without knowing why. They could feel the eyes of the crowd staring at them.

"Don't be so cruel," Aunt Marigold said. "They didn't cause this."

"Oh, Marigold," the Mayor said, shaking his

head in disappointment. "There's nothing else it could be. They're the only thing that's new. Think it through."

Behind him, the children heard someone shout, "Yeah, they're the only thing that's different!"

The Mayor smiled when he heard this, and the crowd seemed to be murmuring in agreement. The Mayor's eyes narrowed, and he stared down at the children.

"Change is always bad, Marigold," he said, not taking his eyes off Connor and Cordelia. "I told you that. I told you to let social services take care of this . . . problem of yours."

"I won't abandon them," Aunt Marigold said quietly. She took one slow step, then another, her ankles shaking slightly, until she stood between the Mayor and the children so that they could no longer see his face.

"Everyone gets abandoned sooner or later," the Mayor said in a low voice. "If your niece and nephew were somehow involved," he went on, louder this time, so everyone could hear him, "we will find out, and we will punish them."

Cordelia and Connor were on the verge of tears. The mention of their parents' death had felt as if someone had hit them in the face, even if no one actually had. Kip was trying to comfort them by rubbing his head up against their legs, one at a time.

"You'll have to prove it first," Aunt Marigold said.

"They're the only new ones, Marigold," the Mayor hissed. "I decide who stays in the town, and when I prove it was them, I'm going to expel them." He stepped to the side so that he could glare at the children. "Think you'll like that? Foster care? You'll probably be split up, sent to different homes, never see each other again."

"Let's go home," Aunt Marigold said. "Mayor, you can handle this problem. You're the one who was supposed to keep track of the crank, after all."

The children looked up at the mention of the crank. It *was* the weapon the Mayor had meant! And they were the ones using it—they were the ones the Mayor wanted to stop. They returned their eyes to the ground, trying not to show their surprise.

Aunt Marigold took both of the children by their hands and led them away from the river and the crowd that was watching them. They could feel the eyes of the crowd and the Mayor on them all the way home.

Chapter 18

W hy don't you children go read?" Aunt Marigold said when they got home. "It'll take your mind off things."

"Did we do something wrong?" Cordelia asked. Everyone, even the Mayor, was asking questions now, so she thought it would be okay to ask another.

"No," Aunt Marigold said, crouching down so she could look them in the eye. "Our town is special, you see. We all decided a long time ago that change is something to be avoided. It usually brings pain. So we figured out a way to keep the town from changing. To keep everything slow and steady. We have our routines, and there are other . . . things, too, that keep everything steady. They're like locks. That way, nothing bad ever happens. The river is supposed to be one of those locks. As long as it doesn't move, the town doesn't change. So people are frightened, is all. They're scared bad things might happen."

"Can't some change be good?" Connor asked.

"Yes," Aunt Marigold said after a moment. "But it can be so bad, too." She looked away, and the children could tell she was remembering something. Maybe it was the phone call she got telling her that her brother was dead. Maybe it was seeing Benny's car crash. "It can be awful. The way we live is safer. You'll see that in time. Now go read. I need to go back. The whole town will be discussing what to do. The Mayor is very angry. I hope you'll forgive him for the horrible things he said."

Aunt Marigold left again, and the children went upstairs. Cordelia pulled out her photo album, and both children stared at the pictures of their parents, forever unchanging in the photos.

"Do you think the Mayor and Aunt Marigold are right?" Cordelia asked her brother. "Do you think it's better if things never change? Our parents wouldn't have died, then, like he said."

"I think," Connor said, rolling onto his back, "that some change is good, and some is bad. And our parents dying was the worst. But before that, they met, and got married, and had us. Those were all changes. None of that could have happened without change. And those were all good things, right?"

"Yeah," Cordelia said.

"Cities are built up over themselves. Time keeps going and people build newer buildings around or on top of the older ones. Or else they become ruins. That's . . . what I know. But those are buildings, towns. I don't know about people."

"I just wish they were still alive. I wish *that* change hadn't happened." Cordelia looked at some more photos, then closed the album. "But I want to change from how we are now, too. I don't want to be this sad forever. Do you think that can change?"

"I think it can if we make it," Connor said, looking his sister in the eye. "I think we should find all the places we can wind the crank."

"But we'll get in trouble," Cordelia said. "We're already in trouble and they don't even know it was us."

"The Mayor knows it was us."

"We can hide the crank. Then he won't know."

"We could . . . but don't you want to use it first? Don't you want to finish what we started?" Connor asked.

Cordelia thought for a moment and looked down at the photo album again. She looked at one photo in particular of her and her brother when she was barely able to talk, and their parents were holding them up in the air. She didn't know who took the picture. Everyone in it looked so happy. She wanted to be that happy again.

"Yes," she said. "Let's finish it."

"If we follow the way the finger is pointing now," Connor said, opening the map on his smartphone, "we should find the next crank spot." He pointed at the statue on the map and drew his finger in a line, showing where it was pointing. This was a part of the map he hadn't drawn yet, a part of the town they hadn't explored.

"Okay," Cordelia said, "so we just need to get to where we think it could be and follow that line, right?"

"Without anyone seeing us," Connor added.

"So we'll be careful. And hopefully, everyone will stay down by the river for a while longer. But we have to hurry."

The children gathered up their things and went to retrieve the crank, too. Cordelia had put it under her bed, but when they looked for it there, she couldn't find it. She reached under and searched with her hand, but found nothing. Connor looked, too, and took out a flashlight. They crawled under the bed, inspecting every corner. But the crank was gone.

Chapter 19

The children felt their blood flow faster and hotter.

"I put it right here," Cordelia said.

"I know, I watched you," Connor said.

"Do you think Aunt Marigold found it?"

"I don't know. We know Gray saw it. . . . He knows we have it. Maybe he took it to give to the Mayor? So we wouldn't get in trouble?"

Cordelia sat down on the floor by her bed, tears welling up in her eyes.

"I felt like we were doing something good."

She sniffled. "I felt like . . . we were supposed to be doing it. Not just 'cause the Mayor is so mean and I want to . . . stop anything he likes. But because . . . I don't know."

"Me too," Connor said, sitting down next to his sister. "I felt that way, too."

"Now it's all gone," Cordelia said. "We're stuck in this stupid town or we'll get sent to foster care and split up or . . . I miss them so much."

"Me too," Connor said. They were both crying a little now, and they spoke in soft, stuttering breaths.

"I felt like . . . when we were making the town better, I felt like I was getting better, too. Like, I was the park, and if it could bloom again, so could I."

"Dad would know what to do," Connor said. "He'd be able to figure out a way to talk to the Mayor and get him to understand that parks should be blooming."

"Or Pop," Cordelia said. "He would play a trick or joke and then the Mayor would be laughing and everyone would think it was so funny that he had tried to stop us in the first place."

They sat like that for a while, next to each other, shoulder-to-shoulder. Kip curled himself up by their feet. Outside, the sky grew darker. The lights weren't on, and it felt as if their room were the only place in the whole world. A wind blew in through the window and sent shivers down their spines.

The wind also blew a folded piece of paper off the nightstand. It landed in front of Cordelia. It was from a notebook, and had little torn holes along the side.

"What's that?" Connor asked, sniffling and wiping tears from his eyes. He was mostly done crying, but not because he wasn't sad. He just didn't feel as though he could cry anymore.

Cordelia reached out for the paper and unfolded it. It was a note.

> Sorry to steal the thing from you, but I need it so I can make the Mayor let my family move into Woundabout. And it was sort of mine to begin with. Don't worry, I'll keep it safe. Cool about the park!
> —Nico

"It wasn't his," Cordelia said. "It was the Mayor's." She suddenly felt angry instead of sad.

"He must have snuck in and stolen it while we were at the river—he's probably not that far ahead of us," Connor said, leaping to his feet.

"But if he tells the Mayor he has it, the Mayor will think he's the one who's been winding everything, and then his family will never be allowed into town!" Cordelia said, also standing. Though moments ago they had been weighed down by sadness, now they felt as though they were vibrating rubber bands. The crank was still out there, but their only friend could get himself in trouble because of what they had done. They had to stop him. And then, maybe . . . they could use the crank again.

"He'll be smart, though. He'll hide it somewhere first so the Mayor can't take it from him before he tells the Mayor he has it. Not the park—that didn't work the first time. Maybe . . . the greenhouses his family runs? Then he'll tell the Mayor he has it, but the Mayor will think it was him doing the winding—and he'll get really mad."

"But then, at least we won't be the ones getting in trouble. . . ."

"Yeah," Connor said. They were afraid of what the Mayor had said, about kicking them out of town, about foster care and being separated. They were all they had left, and they didn't want to lose that. "But . . . we have to at least tell Nico that his plan will backfire."

"So we have to find him. He'll be hiding it. You think in his greenhouses?"

"That's my best guess," Connor said. "It's my only guess."

"Mine too. So let's go."

Chapter 20

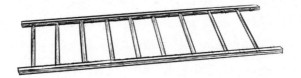

They took the note and all the other things they'd collected and put them in their backpacks. But when they went downstairs, they could see that getting out without anyone seeing them was going to be a problem. Dozens of people had gathered outside the house. They were standing around, their arms crossed, glaring at the house. Aunt Marigold was staring out the window at them.

"Go back upstairs, children," she said when she saw them. "I'll keep them out."

"What do they want?" Cordelia asked.

"I don't know," Aunt Marigold said, her hand fluttering at her neck like a dead leaf in the wind. "I think they just want to search the house—your things. But they won't find the crank, and then it will be fine. Maybe I should just let them search. . . ." She sighed. "I'm not a very good aunt, am I?"

Connor and Cordelia looked at Aunt Marigold's profile as she stared out the window. The light coming in turned her body nearly transparent.

"Sure you are," Connor said.

"Yeah," Cordelia said. "The best."

Aunt Marigold turned to them.

"Thank you," she said. She turned back to look out the window. "I won't let them take you away. Now go back upstairs."

Connor and Cordelia looked at each other and went back upstairs, worried now, not just for themselves and Nico, but for Aunt Marigold, too. They sat together on Connor's bed. Cordelia would have said she felt as though she were trying to take a photo without a lens, and Connor would have said he felt as though he were in a strange city without a map, but they both knew they felt the same thing.

"Aunt Marigold really stood up for us," Cordelia said. Connor nodded. "She's a good aunt," Cordelia went on. Connor nodded again. "We're lucky she took us in. That she loves us like that."

"You think they'd do anything to her?" Connor asked. Cordelia shook her head.

"I don't know," she said. "She's lived here for a long time. I hope not."

"Me too." The children took a deep breath and went into Cordelia's room.

"We need to get out," Cordelia said. She opened the window. There was a tall tree just a few feet away and no one was around. The crowd was at the front of the house.

"That's not safe," Connor said. "We need a way across."

"There's a ladder!" Cordelia said, remembering. She looked at the screen on her camera and flipped through the photos she had taken until she saw the one of the ladder. "It's in the hall closet."

The children took the ladder from the closet, each of them holding one end, and crept down the hall as quietly as they could. They thrust the ladder out Cordelia's window. It landed on the tree's

branch, like a bridge. Connor pushed down on it, testing it to make sure they could get across. Then, holding his breath, he climbed onto the windowsill and crawled across. The ladder didn't fall.

"Come on!" he whispered to his sister. She put Kip on her shoulders and started crawling across, too. But Kip wasn't balanced well and started to fall off her shoulder, dragging her with him.

Cordelia let out a little scream as her right knee and hand came off the ladder. Kip scrambled, and his claws dug into her back. Cordelia looked down at the ground. She wasn't sure if she'd survive the fall, but if she did, she'd definitely break an arm or a leg. Did Woundabout even have a hospital? She hadn't seen one. She clutched the ladder with all her might, but her hands were growing slippery with sweat and she could feel Kip's claws digging into her like knives.

"Hold on!" Connor whispered. The ladder was hard to move from where he was, and heavy because of his sister and Kip. He tried lifting it up on one side, to rock them back into place, like lifting a table to keep a marble from rolling off it, but it wouldn't move. He reached out to where the ladder left the tree and grabbed it there with both hands and pulled it so hard he felt himself starting to tip over. If this didn't work, Cordelia and Kip would fall off the ladder and Connor would fall out of the tree. He squeezed his eyes closed and focused on pulling. His whole body felt hot with the effort of moving the ladder, but finally, he felt it tilt up and shake Cordelia back into a balanced position.

Cordelia felt the ladder ram into her knee as she slid back into place. It was like falling down on the street. She grabbed the ladder as tightly as she could with both hands. Her knee suddenly burned with pain, but she was balanced again and holding tight to the ladder. Kip was just barely hanging on to her by his two front paws. Carefully, she reached out and lifted him back onto her back, where he let out a little sigh of relief. Taking a deep breath, Cordelia finished her climb across to the tree, where Connor still had his eyes closed. She laid her hand on his to let him know they were okay.

"That was close," she said quietly. Connor nodded, opening his eyes.

They climbed down the tree. They peered over the wall but saw no one, so they climbed over it and ran across the street to an alley. They knew they had to be careful. People were looking for them. But they had to warn Nico before he got in trouble because of them.

Chapter 21

It was easy figuring out which way to go—they just had to head downhill. But they were afraid of being found, so they went slowly, carefully, sticking to shadowy alleys and poking their heads around corners before walking out into the street. They stayed far away from the river, and instead walked down the edge of the cliff, where buildings stopped suddenly because the ground stopped. There was no fence, no wall, just a drop right at the edge of the cliff, and the children were careful not to get too close to it.

Luckily, not many people seemed to be out.

They were all still at the river, maybe, or surrounding Aunt Marigold's house. The children's throats went dry when they thought about that, about Aunt Marigold and the trouble she might be in because of them.

They made it to the base of the cliff after a while, and they felt safer there. They weren't in town anymore. No one would be looking for them here.

"There's the train station," Connor said, pointing. "So I'd guess the greenhouses are just beyond it?"

"So let's go," Cordelia said. And they headed down the road, Kip walking beside them.

It was noon when they got to the greenhouses. It had been a long walk. But they weren't tired, because when they saw the greenhouses, they were filled with excitement. Nico hadn't really described them well. He'd just called them greenhouses, but they were more like greenmansions. And so many of them! Palaces made of glass, all filled with green, and glowing like gems in the light. They were close together, with little roads between them, and each of them was shaped differently—this one was a pyramid, that one was a rectangle, and that one looked like the Taj Mahal. It was like a city of crystal. Cordelia immediately began taking photos.

"But how will we find him?" Cordelia asked, her heart sinking.

"I don't know," Connor said.

"Nico!" Cordelia shouted. But there was no response.

"We'll have to check each one," Connor said, looking at the clock on his smartphone. He wondered how long the mob would bother Aunt Marigold, and if they'd eventually leave her alone or storm the house.

"Let's start with this one," Cordelia said, pointing at the one shaped like a dome. Connor nodded, and together they went inside.

The inside of the greenhouse was muggy and hot. The children felt their clothes start to stick to them right away. But it was also beautiful. It was shaped like a circle, and in the circle were rings of raised plant beds, filled with soil and green leafy plants. Above them on the ceiling were sprinklers

that sent down a fine mist. But all of this was nothing next to the robots.

There were three of them. They were hanging from the ceiling by wires, and there were tracks on the ceiling so they could move around. They were spheres, each with arms coming down and a basket hanging underneath, like hot-air balloons. In fact, they resembled hot-air balloons more than they did robots. As the children watched, the robots floated around the room, picking the vegetables—carrots, the children could see once they'd been plucked—from the soil and putting them in their baskets. Then, one of the arms would retract inside the sphere and come back out a moment later, holding a seedling. This it would plant where it had just picked the vegetable. It would gently pat the seedling down, sprinkle some soil over it and water it, and then it would move on to the next.

"Amazing," Connor said. "It's practically

self-sustaining. I guess Nico's family runs this whole place with just these robots."

"Who are you?" came an electronic-sounding voice from the air. The children looked around and saw there was a camera in each of the robots, too. Both robots had stopped what they were doing and were now staring at the children.

"Um, we're looking for Nico," Connor said.

"That's not what I asked," said the voice. It sounded female, despite being electronic and staticky. And it wasn't actually coming from the robots. Connor and Cordelia looked around quickly and spotted a speaker just above the glass doors they'd come through.

"I'm Cordelia," Cordelia said to the speaker, "and this is my brother, Connor. We met Nico in the park two days ago and it's very important we find him. Do you know where he is?"

"Better come see me," the voice said. "I'm in the central building."

"Okay," Connor said.

"So get going," the voice said. "These machines have work to do, and I'm afraid that capybara's fur is going to clog the filters."

The children left the greenhouse the same way they'd come in, and looked around at the village of greenhouses for a central building. But all they could see were more greenhouses.

"Well, it has to be in the center, right?" Connor said, and walked forward.

"Whoever she is," Cordelia said as they walked toward the center of the greenhouses, "she knew what a capybara was."

"Yeah," Connor said. They walked for a while, passing by more and more greenhouses. Some had flowers growing in them; some had trees; some had big, prickly bushes. They all had robots.

"Look," Cordelia said, pressing her face to the glass of the greenhouse with the prickle bushes. "It's picking pineapples." These robots were bigger than the others, and their huge arms easily plucked the pineapples from the center of the bushes and put them in the giant baskets. "They must grow everything here."

"I think I see the central building," Connor said, pointing. Compared to the greenhouses, it didn't look very important—except that it was the only building that wasn't a greenhouse. It was a plain, one-story house with a white picket fence around it. It was painted a light blue and had a gray roof.

"It's certainly something," Cordelia said, disappointed. She thought the central building would be a giant tower of glass. The children approached the house and went through the gate. There was a welcome mat, which they wiped their feet on, and a doorbell, which they rang.

"Come in!" said a voice from inside. The children opened the door. The inside was very plain, with wood floors and white walls. On a small table to the side was a collection of random objects: a pocket watch, a hat with a veil, a wicker basket, and a statue of a winged hippo that looked as if it had once been on a building.

"Think these are other things Nico stole?" Cordelia asked.

"Door on the left," said the voice suddenly. There was a door directly to their left, which they opened. Inside that door, though, things looked entirely different.

The children walked in squinting, because it was so bright. There were screens everywhere, lining all the walls of a giant room. Each screen showed the inside of a greenhouse, but from a robot's point of view, so the camera was moving and shaking. Looking at all the screens at once made the children feel a little seasick.

"Hi," said the voice from earlier. The children realized there had been a person right in front of them the whole time, but with all the screens, they hadn't noticed at first. And she had her back to them. She was sitting in a wheelchair made of shiny chrome. It was a fancier wheelchair than they'd ever seen, like something from the future. And she was typing at a large computer. "Just a sec," she said. She pressed a few keys on the keyboard and turned around. She was older than they were, maybe seventeen, and wore her hair in a ponytail. She smiled, but the children got the impression she was more curious than friendly.

"I'm Ines, Nico's sister. Why are you looking for him?" she said. Her voice wasn't mean, exactly, but she sounded in a hurry to get rid of them.

"He took something," Cordelia said.

"Again?" Ines sighed. "What did he steal from you?"

"No," Connor said. "Not from us. Well, from us, yes, but originally from the Mayor. And he said he was going to tell the Mayor he could only have it back when he let your family move into Wound-about. But if Nico tells the Mayor he has it, he'll get in a lot of trouble . . . 'cause of us."

Ines furrowed her brow and her pale eyebrows came together in a little point over her nose.

"Okay," she said. "Let me . . ." She looked around the room at all the monitors, her head turning in one deliberate swoop, until she stopped at one. "He's burying it in the raspberries," she said. She turned back to her computer and pressed a button and said very clearly, "Nico, get back here. Right. Now."

Nico's voice came through the computer, buzzing with static. "Why?"

"Because you're burying something in the raspberries and I'll tell Mom and Dad who you stole it from if you don't," Ines said.

"Fine," came Nico's angry voice through the static.

"And bring whatever it is you're burying," she said into the microphone. For a moment, a screech of feedback filled the room, but it quickly ended. "Now, then," Ines said, turning back to the children, "did Nico tell you why he wants us to move into Woundabout so badly?"

"He said you'd had an accident," Cordelia said. "And the air would be good for you."

Ines rolled her eyes. "That's what I thought," she said. She sighed again.

"So . . . do you run this place?" Cordelia asked.

"I run the machines," Ines said. "Built them, too. Designed the entire greenhouse system: temperature and humidity control, pollination systems, insect supervision. Dad drives the truck with the fruits and vegetables to sell in Woundabout, and Mom chooses which fruits and vegetables to plant and tells me how they have to be grown, so I can make sure the greenhouse is hot or dry or cold or whatever it needs to be to get the best produce. And Nico . . . steals things."

"That's really awesome!" Cordelia said. "That you built all this."

"Thanks," Ines said. "So . . . how did you come by a capybara?"

"His name is Kip," Connor said. Kip padded over to Ines and sniffed at her wheelchair. Ines bent down and patted him on the head.

"He's cute."

"He belonged to our parents," Cordelia said. "They ran a capybara ranch, but . . ."

"I know," Ines said. "My parents mentioned it. Sorry for your loss." She said it flatly, as though it didn't mean anything, which the children liked, because they knew it didn't. They didn't have to reply. "My parents were angry when they heard you were being allowed to move into town. They've been trying to get in for ages. Something about the air. Nonsense. Weird little town, weird people—no offense. I like the greenhouses way better."

"Yeah," Cordelia said. "I'd rather spend all day here than in Woundabout. It feels more like a home."

"That whole place is weird," Ines said, shaking her head. "I've been up into town three times. That was enough. No internet? No modern tech? It's like they're some outdated machine that won't allow upgrades. Don't get me wrong—I know upgrades can be a hassle, but they make things better. These greenhouses used to operate so slowly. This wheelchair," she said, tapping it, "used to squeak and turn. So I upgraded it."

"It's really cool-looking," Connor said.

"Thanks," Ines said, wheeling closer to them, Kip following so as to continue being petted. "It was hard work, but I'm proud of it." She smiled down at Kip and scratched behind his ears.

"Do you . . ." Cordelia started, but let the question trail off, afraid it was rude.

"What?" Ines asked.

"Is the wheelchair so you can run the robots

better?" Cordelia asked after a moment. "Or do you need it?"

"Both," Ines said. "I was working on a robot—like the ones in the greenhouses—and I made a stupid mathematical error and the balance wasn't right and it fell on me. Stupid, stupid mistake. Sometimes I get so angry at myself when I think about it." She shook her head, and Connor and Cordelia thought about how angry Cordelia had gotten at Kip, even though it wasn't really his fault. "Anyway, spine broke, they tried to fix it, surgery after surgery, until I'd had enough and decided to just move past it, best as I could. All these surgeries and recoveries wasted time I wanted to be doing stuff, y'know? Building robots, going to the movies—I missed twenty-seven movies I wanted to see in the theater 'cause of those surgeries."

"It's so cool how you build robots," Connor said. Cordelia nodded in agreement.

Ines smiled, looking pleased with herself. "Yeah, it is," she said. "My parents moved us here because they wanted to get into Woundabout for its magic air, or whatever, but I moved here because I saw the space to create something amazing out of these greenhouses. And that's what I'm doing."

"So you don't want to move to the town?" Cordelia asked. "Nico said—"

"No. These greenhouses—this tech. That's what I want to be doing. I don't care about the town. Ridiculous." She lifted Kip up into her lap and petted his belly in silence for a few minutes.

Cordelia looked around at the computers and monitors and shiny mechanics and turned back to Ines.

"Do you think . . ." Cordelia started, then paused. "I mean, you're good with machines. So, I guess, do you think trees could be run by machines?"

Ines raised an eyebrow.

"Well, all the trees in the greenhouses are run by machines," she said. "But I'm guessing that's not what you meant." She leaned forward. "Is there a tree machine in town?"

The children stared at her silently and opened their mouths to answer.

"I'm here," Nico interrupted, walking into the room, holding the crank. "Oh, hey, mates," he said, noticing them. "Sorry about the note, but I was in a hurry."

"There you are," Ines said, putting Kip down. "Your friends are here to save you from some trouble, but first you talk to me." She folded her arms across her chest. "What have I said about moving to Woundabout?"

"That you don't want to," Nico said, looking down at the floor.

"Right. So why are you planning on blackmailing the Mayor to get us in?"

Nico kicked the ground silently and let out a long sigh.

"Well?" Ines asked. "Why go to the trouble of stealing from the most important man in town—the man who, by the way, ensures that the town buys our fruits and vegetables?"

Nico wouldn't look up. He mumbled something so softly the children couldn't understand it.

"What?" asked Ines. Nico glanced over at Connor and Cordelia, then back at the ground.

"Because I want it to be like it used to be." He looked up suddenly, his eyes angry and red at the edges. "Why don't you want it to be like it used to be?" he said loudly. He took a step backward, as if he realized how angry he sounded. "Remember when you used to help me make race cars and we'd race down the hill? But now you say it's too much work for you to get up the hill. Or how we used to play catch? Or even how you used to let me help you build the robots? That was fun. Now you kick me out of here if I even touch one."

"I just don't want you to get hurt," Ines said, shaking her head. "I couldn't keep myself from getting hurt—I don't want that to happen to you."

"Yeah," Nico said, looking down, "but I can be careful. And what about the other stuff? We used to . . . have fun. Now you're alone in your lab all day."

"Not all day," Ines said, sounding genuinely surprised. "I go out—you know I've been going on dates with one of the train conductors. . . ."

"Well, you don't hang out with me," Nico said. "You have time for a train conductor, but not me?"

"I . . ." Ines nodded. She glanced at Connor and Cordelia, who turned away, staring at the video monitors so Nico and Ines could have some privacy. "I just thought you didn't want to have anything to do with me now. I mean, how much fun can it be for a kid to hang out with his wheelchair-bound older sister? Isn't that boring?"

"No," Nico said, sounding surprised. "We always have fun together. Remember when we would build forts and make shadow puppets?"

"Yes." Ines smiled. "I remember that. You're right. We should do that. I'm sorry I haven't been fun. But it's not because of my legs. And Wound-about isn't going to fix my legs anyway."

"You don't even want to try?" Nico asked. The children turned their heads slightly, curious about her answer.

Ines tilted her head, thinking. "It's hard," she said. "Wondering if I could undo what happened. And I even tried for that—all those surgeries. But I couldn't keep living like that—hoping to be fixed and always failing. I realized I didn't need to be fixed. I like my life now, Nico. And if I get caught up in thinking, *If only I were more this or more that*, then I'm not going to like my life. I'm just going to wonder about this other life. So, no, I don't want to try. I'm happy. I'm not broken. But I am sorry I haven't been hanging out with you. I'll fix that, I promise."

Connor and Cordelia looked at each other and wondered if they were broken, or whole. Ines made it sound a lot easier than it was. She seemed powerful, maybe kind of bossy, but she built robots and ran a city of greenhouses, and they believed her when she said she was happy. Connor wanted to build cities one day, too, and he knew he wouldn't be able to if he still felt broken when he tried to build them. And Cordelia wanted to have a gallery filled with her photos, and she knew she couldn't take enough new ones to fill that gallery if she just kept looking at all her old ones.

Ines wheeled over to Nico and hugged him.

"Okay," Nico said.

"Now, you need to listen to your friends," Ines said, turning back to Connor and Cordelia. "They have some important stuff to tell you, and were about to tell me something about a tree machine in town."

"We used the crank," Connor blurted out. "On the park, and made it bloom, like you saw, and then on the river. But the Mayor knows it was us and he said he was going to find proof it was us and kick us out, send us to foster care, where we'll be split up."

"So we didn't want you to tell the Mayor you had it—he's so angry he would never let you into Woundabout then," Cordelia finished.

"Oh," Nico said. For a moment his face looked as though he hadn't slept in days, as though he'd just

215

lain in bed, staring at the ceiling, worrying about his sister, and now there was no point in worrying anymore. He took a deep breath. "Thanks, then. Though I guess it doesn't matter," he said quickly, as if he wanted to get it over with. He looked away, out the window at Woundabout. "Why would he be mad about the park blooming, though?"

"And how can a crank make a park bloom?" Ines asked.

"I don't know," Connor said. "Aunt Marigold said it was like a lock that kept things from changing in the town."

"Like a machine!" Ines said, her eyes glowing like her computer screens. "Well, that's my area of expertise."

Chapter 22

S o," Ines said after examining the crank and asking about the holes it went in, "a system of locks to prevent change, a machine that makes flowers bloom—I'd love to see that. It sounds fascinating. You should finish it. Unlock everything else. Get the machine working at full capacity."

"What's 'full capacity'?" Cordelia asked.

"All the way on," Ines said. "That's the best way to test the machine. When you've done that, I can check for unusual signals or currents going into town. I might have to go and find the places where these locks are, though."

"But the Mayor said he'd kick us out if we didn't return the crank," Connor said.

"Tell you what," Ines said. "You get kicked out, you can come stay with us. We have plenty of food, and I could use more hands for some of the machines I'm building. You sound like you're both pretty good with technology. You should come stay here anyway."

"Or," Nico said, "I could return the crank. Put it back in the case in the Mayor's house. Then no one will get in trouble."

"But then we wouldn't get to see what the machine does," Ines said. "And everything the crank has done so far is good. I can't imagine the machine is a bad thing. It allows change. It's like with my robots—I tinker with them and change them and make them better. Sometimes I accidentally make things worse, or break things. . . ." She trailed off for a moment, her eyes far away. "But that doesn't matter," she continued, shaking her head. "I fix it. I learn from my mistakes. My robots get better. Besides, you can't really stop it. The town didn't stop change—I mean, you're here. They're just hiding from it. That's not the same."

Connor and Cordelia thought about the recent changes in their own lives—the deaths of their parents, coming to Woundabout. Their lives, they knew, would be better if those changes hadn't happened. But then they also would never have really met Aunt Marigold, never seen the trees in the park explode with petals. If change really was unavoidable, they were glad it wasn't all bad. Connor would have said that even if a building collapsed, and it had been a beautiful building, at least they could build another. And Cordelia would have said that even if a photo came out all wrong, it could still be a breathtaking picture.

Ines turned to the children, and they looked up at her, focusing on the present. "Turn on the machine. Find the next place for the crank."

"We don't know where it is," Cordelia said. "We just sort of know where the statue was pointing."

"You have a photo of the statue on that camera?" Ines asked. Cordelia nodded. "And you've
been mapping on your smartphone?"

"Yes," Connor said.

"Hand 'em over," Ines said, reaching out. Slowly,
the children gave her their gadgets. Ines turned
back to her computers and, in a flurry of plugs and

typing, connected the devices. The screens around the room started showing the photos Cordelia had taken and the map Connor had drawn. They flicked back and forth, like some sort of code, until finally they settled down. Spread out over all the monitors on one wall was a photo of the statue pointing, and Connor's map.

"This dot here," Ines said, pointing at the map. "That's the statue?" Connor nodded. Ines typed a few more things into her computer. "Then, there," she said, a red dot appearing on Connor's map. "That's where another winding spot will be . . . except . . ." Ines turned back to the computer and tapped her finger on her chin a few times. "Yeah, that's where it is, but it's underground. If the statue is pointing correctly, anyway."

"Underground?" Cordelia asked.

"I know where it is!" Nico shouted suddenly. "The sewers!"

"The sewers?" Connor echoed. Sewers were usually disgusting and filled with rats and the things you flush down toilets.

"I use them to get places when I don't want to

be seen," Nico said. "To lift stuff. They're real nice. Walkways, tiles. It's like they used to be used for, like, strolling or something. And we can use them to get to the Mayor's house, too. To put the crank back. If you don't want to find the last winding spot."

Connor and Cordelia looked at each other, unsure of what to do.

"Well, I guess we could at least go to the sewers," Connor said. "We can decide what to do as we walk." Cordelia nodded in agreement.

"Okay, then," Nico said. "Follow me."

"Turn it back on," Ines barked at Connor and Cordelia as she handed back the camera and phone. "I want to know what it does."

"Thanks," Cordelia said after a moment. "For everything."

"You want to come?" Connor asked.

"I do . . ." Ines said, looking back and forth between her monitors and the crank. "But I really can't. Got greenhouses to run. But come back and get me when you've turned it on. I'll set the green-houses up so they can run without me for a while." She turned back around to her computer, giving Kip one more pat on the head as she did so.

Feeling as though they'd just been dismissed, the children and Nico left the house, Nico leading the way toward Woundabout and the sewers.

Chapter 23

Nico led them through the village of green-houses and back toward Woundabout.

"Sorry I got you in trouble," he said as they walked.

"It's not your fault," Connor said. "It's ours, for using the crank."

"It's the Mayor's," Cordelia said. "All these silly rules, these routines. . . . We should find the next place to wind the crank. Just to show him he can't control other people's lives."

"But what if they split us up?" Connor asked. "Put us in foster care?"

"Then we'll run away. Ines said we could stay with them."

"Ines and Nico's parents might not like that," Connor pointed out.

"Eh, we could hide you," Nico said. "Bring you food. It'd be ages before anyone found out."

They walked on in silence for a while longer, until they passed the train station and were near the edge of town.

"It's here," Nico said. He led them off the main road to a small river. The river came out of a tunnel. "These are the sewers. I don't, like, have them

memorized or anything, but it's just like above. If you know where you want to go, you can probably figure it out. Just look for a manhole cover."

"Won't those be heavy?" Cordelia asked.

"Nah," Nico said. "They're all wood for some reason. Fancy, coated in plastic stuff, but easy to lift. And they have the word *vote* carved into them. It's weird."

"This whole town is weird," Cordelia said.

"You still have your flashlight?" Connor asked.

"Yes," Cordelia said. "I'm digging it out."

It was pitch-black under the city; so dark they could feel it. It smelled like old, stale water that hadn't moved in forever. But the water was moving now—they could hear it, murmuring like a thousand people whispering different things all at once. Like a thousand secrets.

They both clicked their flashlights on at the same time, lighting up the sewer they were in. It wasn't the filthy mess they'd expected. Instead, they were on a tiled platform, and next to them was the water, running like a river. The tunnel was curved in an arch over them, but it was large. It was tiled, too, in a checkerboard pattern of dark green and maroon. Cordelia took photos, and the flashes lit up the whole tunnel for a moment, making the colors glow. It felt almost like a palace under the city.

As they walked farther along, heading toward the red dot Ines had marked on Connor's map, they noticed that in some places there were pieces of paper taped to the walls.

"What do they say?" Cordelia asked, taking Kip off her shoulders and setting him down on the ground. Kip sniffed the ground a few moments, then jumped into the river.

"Kip, that water is filthy," Connor said. But Kip didn't seem to mind. The children sighed and turned back to the papers taped to the walls. They were yellowed with age, and the corners were curling inward, but they were clearly campaign posters—the sort people put up when they're running for something; in this case, Mayor.

VOTE FOR ME AND LIVE FOREVER, the first poster said, over a photo of the Mayor. HECTOR STILLMAN.

"Is Hector Stillman the Mayor's name?" Cordelia asked. "And what does he mean, live forever?"

"And why would there be a campaign poster in

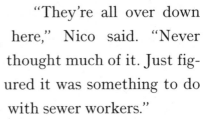

the sewer?" Connor asked.

"They're all over down here," Nico said. "Never thought much of it. Just figured it was something to do with sewer workers."

"Here's another one," Cordelia said, shining her flashlight a little ahead.

WITH MACKENROTH GRAY THERE'S NOTHING TO FEAR, said the poster, right over a picture of Gray, looking almost exactly the same as he did today, except his neutral expression was replaced by one of pride, his chest puffed out as he looked up and to the left, at the curling yellow corner of the poster.

"These must be from when Gray was running for Mayor," Connor said.

"He looks so powerful in the poster," Cordelia said. "Do you think he didn't tell anyone about the crank because he wanted to be Mayor, but wasn't?" she asked, shining her light on Kip, who was still splashing happily in the water.

Connor shrugged. "I feel even more confused about this place now," he said. "These underground posters. And the Mayor promising people they could live forever? That has to be a lie. How did he get elected?"

"Aunt Marigold said the town had a way to keep itself from changing," Cordelia said.

"And my parents say no one gets sick here," Nico added.

"I don't understand how a crank can control . . . time," Cordelia said. "The weather changes! It was raining when we got here."

"That's true," Connor said.

They walked farther along, the tunnel leading them straight ahead. Kip swam alongside them in the filthy sewer water. Connor was just happy it wasn't sewage of the toilet kind. There were more of the same posters on the wall as they walked. In a few places, the tunnel connected with other tunnels—but these were just filled with water, and didn't have a place to walk.

After a while, they came to an archway in the wall. The tunnel continued one way, but the golden arch in the wall stood out, as though it was special somehow. Posters were taped up everywhere around it, one over another over another, as if Gray and the Mayor had been waiting here side by side, and the moment one put up a poster, the other tried to cover it with his own. Beyond the arch it was dark, though. Cordelia took a photo of the archway, and for a moment they could see a big open room, with what looked like an altar in its center. Connor looked down at his map. They were right on top of the red dot.

They walked through the arch. There was no water here. Kip got out of the water to follow them, now smelling musty.

The children shone their flashlights around the room. It was a big room, with a vaulted ceiling, but

it clearly hadn't been used in a very long time. Old cardboard boxes were piled up against the walls in towers that looked as though they might crash down at any moment. In the center of the room was what looked like a giant birdbath made from carved stone. On one side, the rim stuck out like a balcony for squirrels; on the balcony was a black box with a small slot in the lid.

"It looks like a ballot box," Connor said. "Like when we vote for class president."

"Do you think this is where they voted for Mayor?"

"Why would they vote underneath the city?" Connor asked.

"I wish we could turn on the lights," Cordelia said. Kip, still soggy, head-butted her leg. "Ew, Kip. Wait till you're dry before cuddling." But Kip didn't seem to want to cuddle. Instead he walked away from her, looking over his shoulder at the children. They followed him around the birdbath to the other side. There was another small balcony on the rim. Cordelia shone her flashlight on it. This one didn't have a ballot box. It had a small hole. For the crank.

"Should we?" Connor asked.

"I can return it," Nico said again. "So you won't get in trouble."

Cordelia didn't say anything. She grabbed the crank out of her brother's bag, stuck it into the hole, and began to turn it. No one stopped her. Connor reached out and helped his sister turn the crank. From the bottom of the birdbath, stretching up like a telescope, came flames. The children quickly pulled their hands away, but when the flames stayed small and at the bottom of the bowl, they started turning the crank again. The fire slowly grew, reaching upward until it was so big the children had to stop. But the fire didn't stop. It filled the birdbath, crackling and roaring, and lighting up the room. In response, other lights around the room that the children hadn't seen in the dark flickered awake. There was a chandelier above them, and all the candles on it sparked into life. There were torches at the corners of the walls that began burning. The children looked around, suddenly nervous—all the old boxes and papers were still crowding the room. What if they set fire to the place? But the boxes and papers had been left far from the torches.

The whole room was lit up now, glowing and warm. They could see everything clearly—it was a giant room, with the birdbath in the center. The birdbath wasn't just marble, as they had thought, but something paler, like ivory, and it didn't blacken where the flames touched it. And the floor, which they hadn't looked at, was made of glass panes. Under the glass were gears, slowly rotating. They

made a clanking sound that echoed everywhere, as if they were in the heart of a machine.

"Look!" Cordelia said, pointing at where the walls reflected the fire back in strange colors. "There's something on the walls behind the boxes."

Chapter 24

The children quickly began taking down the towers of boxes, carefully putting them where they couldn't catch fire. The boxes were light, and it didn't take long for them to reveal that on each wall of the room was a giant mosaic, made of pieces of tile in deep, vibrant colors like the gemstones on a crown. Though they were covered in dust and hadn't been polished in years, the mosaics still glowed in the firelight. Cordelia immediately began taking pictures.

"Look," Connor said. "There are words at the bottom."

THE ELEMENTS
OF THE
MOUNTAIN

Together, the words and pictures told a story, which the children read:

Once, when the world was young, the elements flew about, making sure they could touch every place on earth. Air brought wind and rain, Water made rivers flow, Earth made mountains rise and plants bloom, and Fire brought light and heat. They danced over the world, bringing their gifts everywhere they went. Until they came to a cliff. As they were bringing their gifts to the cliff, the cliff said:

"No."

The elements stopped. They didn't know what the cliff meant.

"No?" asked Air.

"I don't want you here. Leave me alone," said the cliff.

"But we bring life," Earth said.

"No, you don't," said the cliff. "Things that bloom wither and die. Water can flood, fire can burn, and wind can knock things over. I don't want any of that."

"But you need water to drink," said Water, nearly crying.

"And air to breathe," said Air.

"I bring heat and light!" said Fire angrily. She couldn't believe anyone would say no to her.

"And I bring trees and flowers," Earth said. "Yes, they die, but they grow again in the spring."

"I want to be left alone," said the cliff. The elements all stared at it awhile, hoping it would change its mind. But it didn't. Earth left first, with a sigh. She had been told no before, by deserts and by Antarctica, where nothing grew, but never by a cliff. Fire crossed her arms and stormed off, still offended. Water left, crying. But Air stayed where he was, smiling.

"The others might go," Air said, "but you can't get rid of me. I'm everywhere. And because you were so mean to my brother and sisters, I'm going to make sure I blow extra hard on you. You'll be one of the windiest cliffs in the world."

And Air made good on his promise. He blew and blew, and the cliff begged him to stop, but he wouldn't. And to this day, the cliff is one of the windiest cliffs in the world, but none of the other elements will visit it.

The children stopped reading and looked at one another.

"It's just a story," Connor said. "It can't be real, right?"

"The top of the city, by the Mayor's house, *is* awfully windy," Cordelia said.

"It's true," said a voice behind them. The children and Kip jumped at the sound and turned, afraid the Mayor had found them. But it was Gray. "The story is true."

Chapter 25

The children stared at Gray, a hundred questions bubbling on their lips.

"But what about the park?" Cordelia asked.

"Did you let us take the crank because you're not Mayor?" Connor asked.

"Will people really not get sick here?" Nico asked.

"Why did the Mayor tell people they could live forever?"

"What about the river?"

Gray held up both his hands, and the children went silent.

"When people moved here," Gray explained, "all they had was the wind. But we need other things to live—we need plants and water and fire. So they built a machine. A big one, all gears and cogs under the city, that brought the gifts of the other elements onto the cliff, like a train brings people.

The gears pull water and earth and fire into town. Then they can exist here, too."

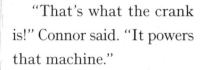

"That's what the crank is!" Connor said. "It powers that machine."

"Just like my sister said," Nico added.

"But then why was it off?" Cordelia asked.

"It was a theory of our current Mayor, when he was young. As an experiment, he asked the town to let the machine wind down for a week. Before then, he planted two flowers, one inside town, one just outside, on either side of the town line. After the week was up, the flower in town hadn't grown at all, and the flower outside of town was in full bloom. He said he thought that without change, people could live forever. No one was sure if he was right at the time, but then he grew up and explored the world. He found other strange spots across the globe, places where an element or two or three were missing, and he studied how they affected those places. He came back confident— if sick. He said if we turned off the machine, if we stopped change, we'd all be well forever. We wouldn't change. No sickness, no death, no strange new ideas. He ran for Mayor on that. And when he won, he let the machine wind down and proved he was right. Woundabout stopped changing. And without change, there's nothing to fear. Or so the Mayor says. But he's dying. Or was dying. He was very sick when he ran for Mayor. He used people's fear of change to win. Of course, you can't stop all change. People's minds, new arrivals, like you. But the seasons, disease—they're frozen here. Time even moves slower. As long as the elements are kept away, people live longer, diseases kill slower, and people can keep the outside far away and try not to let anything else new happen."

"You're not afraid of change?" Cordelia asked.

"No," Gray said. "Are you?"

"Sometimes," Connor said. Cordelia nodded in agreement.

Gray smiled down on them. It was a soft sort of smile, as though he was happy and sad at the same time. He looked up at the murals. "I was married once. Her name was Miranda. She left me. I know how bad change can be—how much it can hurt. But I also know that change is what got me past that. What helped me to be happy again." He looked back at the children. "I think you children are change like that. You've made Marigold so happy."

"We have?"

"Oh, yes," Gray said, sitting down on the dirty floor. He crossed his legs as he spoke. "She may be afraid to show it—afraid of violating the Mayor's ridiculous laws—but she's been so lonely. You're her family." Gray's eyes were now level with their own, and though they were plain, and difficult to describe, they were filled with a warm fire that let the children know he was telling the truth.

Connor and Cordelia looked at each other. They

thought about how Aunt Marigold had promised to protect them and had stood in front of the Mayor when he'd looked as if he wanted to hit them. She'd never let them be separated, as the Mayor had said. She'd keep them safe. They suddenly wished she were here with them.

Gray spread his arms wide, taking in the glowing room. "This used to be a special place. People would speak about the town, how we could improve it, make it better. This chamber is closest to the machine that draws in the elements, you see"—he pointed at the gears under their feet—"so it's closest to the machine that makes our city unique. That was the idea—a meeting hall where we could remember why we were special and how we should keep being special."

Gray dropped his arms. "It was fifteen years ago. Just around when your parents got married, just after Benny Banai died in the car crash, because that was when Marigold moved to town. She was so afraid of the world back then. Afraid of more loss." Gray pushed himself to his feet and dusted off his pants with his hands. "Things in the world were changing, and people weren't sure what to think of it. The Mayor told them it was bad, that we had to preserve our way of life. I told them change was nothing to fear and we should focus on other things, like schools and parks. They believed him. We stopped winding the machine—though it had been wound since the eighteen hundreds. The machine wound down. Things . . . stopped."

Gray walked back and forth, studying the murals on the walls. His expression was sad, and tired. "When the Mayor was elected, people stopped coming here. He stopped having town halls. He wanted to stop people from talking about things. He told them too many questions, too many ideas, would bring change back. He told us to stick to routines, and keep outsiders out. Move the children away—because children cause more unpredictable changes than adults. We don't even have a town paper anymore, or get the news on the television. But now you've gone and started winding things." His voice grew less neutral as he spoke, almost happy at the end, as though he and the children were in on a private joke.

"So, what about the rest of the town?" Connor asked. "Is everyone mad at us for changing things?"

Gray knelt down so the children could see into his eyes. "No," he said. "I'm very happy that you found the crank and have used it and want things to change again. And so are many of the other townspeople. So not everyone is angry. But some are. But if you want, you can tell them it was my fault. I let you take the crank. I knew what it would do."

"Why did you?" Connor asked.

"Because I thought that if children could change the town, then it was time for the town to change. You're what the town needs. The crank is just what you're using to get the job done. I . . . should be doing it myself. But I've been afraid to, all this time. Afraid of getting kicked out. I don't want to go, you see. I love it here. I love . . ." He looked at the children and paused. "The town," he finished. Connor and Cordelia thought he was probably going to say something else, but weren't sure what.

"We're afraid, too," Cordelia said. "Aunt Marigold is our only family, and the Mayor said we'd be sent to foster care and split up." They stared at Gray in silence, and Gray looked down at his shoes. The fire crackled in the torches, and the sound of it echoed in the room, a little like the sound of the rain on the street when they'd first come to Woundabout.

"But we did it anyway," Connor said. "Because we had to." He looked at his sister, who nodded in agreement.

"I know. You've done such a good job so far," Gray said, staring at the murals again. "Better than I could have."

"So far?" Connor asked. "But the job is done. The story said it was only earth, water, and fire that went away."

"Right," Cordelia said, realizing all the things

they'd wound. "We wound earth in the park. It made the flowers and trees bloom. That was one lock."

"Water in the river," Connor said. "Real, fresh, running water. That was the second lock."

"And fire just now," Cordelia said. "The last lock. We're done. Things should be changing now."

"They are," Gray said, "but slowly. And they'll wind down again. If you want the town to stay changed . . . there's one more thing you have to wind. The windmill."

"What windmill?" Nico asked. "Woundabout doesn't have a windmill. We would have seen it."

"The Mayor's house!" Connor said suddenly. Gray nodded. "The Mayor's house is the only place that makes sense. It's so windy up there."

"If you start up the windmill," Gray said, "it will power all the other elements, now that the machine has started. It keeps everything working, and we have to wind only it—and just once a year. As long as the wind blows and the windmill stays open, this town will be like any other."

Connor and Cordelia looked at each other and,

without saying anything, took each other's hands. They knew they had to finish this. Connor would have said it was like the need to keep building a town up, even after an earthquake hits, and Cordelia would have said it was like the need to keep taking photos until you got that perfect shot, no matter how long it took, but they knew they were feeling the same thing. They needed to finish what they'd started, and bring change to Woundabout.

"So we have to get to the Mayor's house," Connor said. "There was a manhole in the middle of the square in front. Can these tunnels take us there?"

"Yes," said Gray, "but be careful. Now that you've turned the fire crank, people will feel the change. They'll know you're down here. They're probably waiting at all the manholes in town. I'll go ahead and try to distract them. I'll rally the townsfolk who do want change. But be quick. Don't let anyone stop you."

"I'm going to slip off," Nico said, "if you're going to turn the last one. I'm another kid—I'll run around the sewers splashing and such, and they'll think I'm one of you and chase after me."

"Won't you get in trouble?" Cordelia asked.

Nico shrugged. "Not much more than usual," he said with a grin.

"Thanks," Connor said. "But be careful, too."

"We don't want anyone to get caught," Cordelia said.

"Don't worry about me," Nico said, waving his arm. "No one's caught me yet."

"Okay," Cordelia said. "Thank you."

She looked at her brother. Both of their mouths were straight lines of determination. They knew they needed to do this. They needed things to change, because if they didn't . . . then they'd always be like this. They'd always feel draped in sadness. And that would be more awful than anything that change could bring.

Chapter 26

Everyone, be very careful," Cordelia said to the assembled group. They were going to split up, and they each had a dangerous mission: Connor and Cordelia, to get to the Mayor's house and wind the crank there; Nico, to distract the townsfolk looking for Connor and Cordelia in the sewers; and Gray, to rally the other townsfolk and get them to look at change as a good thing. It wasn't going to be easy, and if any of them were caught, they might not see the others again.

"No worries," Nico said, and looked as though he was about to dash out, but Cordelia hugged him before he could. Connor hugged him, too, and Nico's eyes shone brightly when the hugs were done. "I haven't had many pals," he said. "Not since we came here, I mean. I'm all isolated with the greenhouses and such. But I'm glad to have met you two." He raised his hand to his forehead and saluted them before winking and running out into the sewers.

The children were left alone with Gray, who knelt down to look them in the eye. "You are the best thing that has happened to this town, and to your aunt Marigold," he said. "And to me," he added, as if surprised by it. "Be careful. You've made it this far."

"You too," Connor said. "Don't get in any trouble because of us."

"I won't," said Gray, standing up and pushing his shoulders back. He marched out into the sewers, leaving Connor and Cordelia alone in the room. Connor stared down at the gears rotating under their feet. Cordelia looked up at the murals that surrounded them.

"Well," she said after a moment, "we should get going."

"Yeah," Connor said, and reached out his hand again. Cordelia took it, and together they walked out into the sewers and headed forward in the darkness, Kip alongside them.

They walked with purpose, but they still had trouble navigating. Connor mapped the sewers as best he could and guessed which way they had to turn, from his experience with maps and from knowing which way the windmill was. It was cold, but they were nervous, and that made them warmer when they knew they should be shivering. The walls of the sewers were wet with beads of liquid, and there was always the sound of dribbling water.

Sometimes they stopped and turned off their flashlights as they heard footsteps, or low voices calling, "You see anything?" Once, a manhole opened just a few feet from them, and the shadow of a head looking down was cast right by their feet. They froze, afraid to breathe.

"Any children down there?" said a hoarse voice. Connor and Cordelia stayed silent. "Nothing here," the voice said, and the manhole cover closed back up again. They were scared, damp with sweat, and the sewer smelled like rotting food and fungus. Even Kip was nervous, and wouldn't go back into the water.

They held hands as they walked. They remembered how their parents had told them they were a family and they would always be together, and as long as they were together, they could do anything.

"We have your auntie, kiddies," said a voice in the darkness. The children froze and held their breaths. "Come out now and we won't hurt her." In the darkness they could hear only the running water.

"They're not here," said another voice. "Let's try this way." The children heard footsteps heading off in another direction, and they exhaled.

"Think they'll really hurt her?" Cordelia whispered. She imagined Aunt Marigold in a dark room somewhere, tied to a chair, crying.

"I don't know," Connor said, and shivered. "I hope not."

"What if they do, though?" Cordelia whispered. "What if they have her in the trunk of a car or a basement with rats? She was trying to protect

us." Cordelia's voice got louder as she said this, and she realized it and stopped talking. She took a deep breath and tried to calm herself, but her heart was beating so quickly and loudly she was sure people could hear it throughout the sewers.

"I don't think the Mayor will, though," Connor said. "Not until he's found us. If they hurt her before, then we'd just get angry and not give him the crank. He'd wait until we could see him hurting her."

"Okay," Cordelia said, although she didn't feel reassured. She squeezed her brother's hand in the darkness, and he squeezed back. "We'll save her, then," Cordelia whispered.

"Yes, we will. Let's go."

Connor led the way. There were some turns and intersections, but Connor knew they just needed to keep heading up, and that was easy. When they got to a manhole cover at a dead end, they knew it was the right one because they could hear the wind whipping over it on the other side.

"Are you ready?" Connor asked his sister. She nodded.

"Are you?" she asked. He nodded. They both knew they were nervous. So they looked each other in the eye and climbed up the ladder.

Chapter 27

They slid the manhole cover open, expecting to be swarmed by angry townsfolk, but there was no one there. They crawled out slowly, but the plaza was empty, apart from the wind. The children felt their hair and clothes being blown around, and heard the loud whistling of air past their ears. Leaves flew in small circles and suddenly dived off the cliff. Kip was having trouble keeping his footing and stayed close to the children, using them as a shield from the gusts.

They stared up at the house. It was old, and the tower was bent over slightly. They wondered how it wasn't more damaged after being blown by the wind for so many years.

They looked down at the town—and they immediately ducked. There were all the townspeople. Just below them, in front of the square, where it wasn't so windy. Gray and the Mayor were arguing, and everyone was staring at them. No one had noticed the children. Yet. So they stayed low to the ground and crawled away from the crowd.

"Where do you think the hole is for the crank?" Connor shouted over the wind, hoping his voice wasn't carried down to the townsfolk.

"I don't know," Cordelia shouted back, looking

around for a hole. The wind blew dust in her eyes and she had to look down and blink it away before she could open them again.

Kip nudged Connor's leg and looked at the side of the house, under the tower.

"Over there," Connor said, heading toward where Kip was leading them. Kip stayed close so as not to get blown away, but when they got close to the tower, he started sniffing anxiously at the wind, and pointed his head toward a large stone that was at the edge of the cliff. The children walked toward it very slowly.

"Be careful," Cordelia said. "I don't want to get blown off the cliff."

The hole was just behind the rock, a few feet from the edge. Connor started to get the crank out of his bag, but turned as he heard the sudden roar of the crowd behind him. The townsfolk had spotted them, and the Mayor was leading them in a charge up the hill, his face red with anger. He was screaming something the children couldn't make out, and new wrinkles seemed to be appearing in his face like rippling sheets.

"Quick!" Cordelia shouted as she took the crank from Connor and shoved it into the hole. The children started to wind the crank as quickly as they could, which was hard, since they were pushing it against the wind. Cordelia looked back and saw the Mayor was almost there, stomping his feet, his hands balled up into fists. Gray was chasing after

him, though, and grabbed him by the shoulder. The Mayor turned and pushed Gray with both arms, sending him rolling back down the hill. The Mayor spun back to the children and started running toward them.

"Faster," Cordelia said, and they wound the crank again.

"I knew it was you!" the Mayor screamed, finally upon them. He grabbed the crank, but the children kept pushing it. They wound it one more time before the Mayor grabbed it and pulled it from the ground, holding it above him like a club. He looked as if he was about to hit Connor with it and knock him back over the cliff, but suddenly there was a sound above them, and they all looked up.

The tower had straightened itself out, and a bar had emerged from the side of it. With a pop, the bar opened like an umbrella, creating a small wooden circle, and from that circle came four more bars extending outward.

"No!" screamed the Mayor.

The circle began to move, and as it did so, the four bars moved with it, leaving trails in the air.

But they weren't just trails, the children realized. They were sails. The tower had become the windmill, and it was spinning in the wind. It spun a few times and the ground shook a little under their feet. The children grabbed onto each other, afraid of falling off the cliff.

The Mayor's arms fell to his sides like a puppet's without strings. The crank dropped from his hand with a dull thud. He looked down at them, and he didn't look angry anymore. He looked tired, and pale. He tried to take a step but tottered slightly. He took another step, stumbling back toward the windmill. As he leaned against it, his hands spread out, trying to find something to keep him upright. They found a window latch, but instead of keeping him steady, it fell open as he pulled. The wind picked up, and suddenly, like a tornado, all the Mayor's postcards came flying out the window and over the cliff.

"No!" the Mayor cried out. He let go of the window and seemed to have enough strength to take a step forward, reaching out for the postcards, which were dancing in circles just beyond the edge of the

cliff. He fell to his knees, still reaching. "Please," he said in a soft voice. "Please. All I wanted was my sister to come visit me again. All she sends are those postcards." The postcards, or maybe the wind, seemed to hear him, because all the post-cards flew back to him, surrounding him in a spiral before landing around him in a circle. "I didn't want to die alone," he said. And then he collapsed, the postcards like a bed of flower petals. The wind-mill creaked above them. Connor and Cordelia just stared at him, afraid to speak.

Gray rushed over to the Mayor and put his ear to the man's chest.

"He's still alive," he called to the crowd. "Someone get him to the hospital."

Immediately, several others from the crowd ran forward and hefted the Mayor's body up and ran him downhill, out of sight. The children stared after them, worried that they had just killed him. Gray came over and laid a hand on their shoulders.

"We'll do everything we can," he said.

"Did we do that?" Cordelia asked. "Is he going to die? Did we kill him?"

"No," Gray said. "He was dying anyway. The town just . . . held him for a while. But you didn't kill him. What you did was all this." Gray gestured at the town, and the children looked out over it. Flowers were blooming suddenly out of the grass. Bare trees were exploding with leaves. There were birds and kites in the sky. The wind went from hurricane levels to a gentle breeze, and the noise it made almost vanished completely. Everyone who had been watching them was now watching

271

the town, and the children could hear them oohing and aahing.

Aunt Marigold turned away from the town and looked at the children. She walked toward them, and they stood up to meet her. They were afraid of what they had done. They were afraid they were going to be punished. Aunt Marigold didn't look angry, though. She was smiling. And she seemed a little older. Her blond hair had streaks of white in it they hadn't noticed before.

"Oh, children," she said when she was close to them. She sounded as though she thought it was funny. "You brought change back to Wound-about."

"Then why aren't you mad?" Connor asked. "I thought you said it was better if things didn't change."

Aunt Marigold took a deep breath and exhaled slowly, as if she was trying to get up the courage to say something. "I was afraid," she finally said. "When Benny died, it was . . . horrible. It took a week. I watched him dying for a week—I lived through that, and afterward, I knew I never wanted to experience it again. My brother—your dad—had already met Adam, and they were married and starting a new life. They said I could come stay with them, but they were doing so many new things—opening a ranch, having children. I thought, *What if something goes wrong?* I was so scared. Of being alone, of more people leaving, of new people coming into my life and then leaving again. So I came here, far from the world. It was during the election, and the Mayor talked about a world where nothing ever changed, and that sounded wonderful. I voted for him. Except you can't stop change. Bad things did happen. Awful things. My brother—your parents—are dead. I couldn't stop that by moving here. Life is still going on, and I can't hide my head in the sand and hope nothing bad ever happens again. And neither can you. You shouldn't. I knew it when I first saw you. I knew change was inescapable. And having you in my life . . . that's a good change for me. Having family again. I'd forgotten how good change could be until I saw you, and your flappy panda—"

"He's a capybara," Cordelia corrected.

"Right. A capybara. And seeing you made me so happy . . . and I realized I hadn't felt that way in a long time."

"So we did the right thing?" Cordelia said. Aunt Marigold looked behind her at the crowd of townspeople who had gathered. They were staring up at the windmill. Some looked angry, but most of them were smiling, as though they finally felt relaxed after years of being uneasy.

"Oh, yes," Aunt Marigold said, and knelt down and hugged both of them. It was a warm, close hug, like a favorite sweater. And the children suddenly felt as though they were finally home.

"Things are going to be different now," Gray said

to the town. He was standing in front of the Mayor's house, and he looked as though he belonged there. "Some of you may not like it." And indeed, many of the townsfolk were frowning and grumbling. Some were glaring at the children. "But the windmill has been reactivated. Which means we'll be changing for at least another year, before the windmill needs to be rewound. And I think that's a good thing."

"Me too!" shouted someone from the crowd. Gray smiled.

"Let's think of this as a test. If, in a year, the majority of you want to go back to your old lives, we can let the windmill wind down. But if you find the coming year is good, and I think you will, then we can wind it up again."

"What about the children?" someone shouted.

"No one will hurt them," Gray said. "They did what children do. They changed things. It's in their nature. Let's see if we can be as strong as the children."

Some in the crowd grumbled again, but no one wanted to fight Gray.

"We can stop our old routines!" Mrs. Washburn said. "I can get an electric dryer!" She grinned from ear to ear. And other townsfolk, realizing how they could change their lives for the better, started to smile, too. Gray folded his arms and looked at them, pleased.

"So let's try this out," he said. "Everyone with me?"

The townspeople all looked at Gray and nodded. Some of them looked frightened. Some looked thrilled. The children didn't know what any of it meant, but they felt good, somehow, as if they'd done the right thing.

Gray turned away from the townspeople and walked up to the children.

"They'll see it's better this way," he whispered to Aunt Marigold. "We can become better this way, if we work toward it. The other way, we couldn't become anything."

Nico suddenly bolted out of the crowd and ran up to Connor and Cordelia.

"You did it, mates!" he said. "Real impressive. Ines's gonna be sad she missed it. But then she'll

be out here to study the machine in no time, I'll bet. And I played no small part, I'm proud to say. I had a dozen or so of 'em chasing me around the sewers thinking I was you. I led them on a real fun ride."

"Thanks," Connor said.

"Yeah, thank you," Cordelia said. "If you hadn't stolen the crank in the first place . . ." She looked over to where the crank was, fallen by the side of the Mayor's house. "What do we do with the crank now?"

"I'll take care of it," Gray said. "I'll put it somewhere safe."

The children walked over to the crank and stared down at it. It wasn't very impressive. Just metal bent the right way. But it was magic, too. They leaned down and together took it off the ground and handed it to Gray. They thought that if this were a story, this would be the ending. But endings don't really happen, because an ending means everything stayed the same forever, and the children knew now that they didn't ever want that.

Acknowledgments

We have so many people to thank, but first and foremost we'd like to thank our family for all their support. Especially Mom, not just for her reading it over and over, but also for her insistence that a capybara would make a great children's companion. Also, Meghan, for her encouragement and for her weird childhood games, and Chris, for his insights into the field of writing for a younger audience.

We owe so much to our agent, Joy, as well as Luke and the whole team at David Black. Thank you guys so much for constantly looking out for us.

This book would not have happened without our editor, Alvina, who took the time to really show us what a middle grade book was, even when it was clear we had no idea what we were doing. She taught us so much over the course of this project and took what was essentially just an idea and helped us shape it into a book. We would have been totally lost without her. We cannot say thank-you enough. And so many thanks to the rest of our team at Little, Brown: Bethany, Nikki, Christine, Jennifer, Jenny, Faye, and all the rest for all the hard work and crafting of this book. Special thanks to Tracy for being so amazing and visionary with all the art—especially the cover, which we had some trouble with. And special thanks to Victoria, not just for all her hard work on the book but also for her amazing company and friendship.

Lev would particularly like to thank Robin, Robin (both of them), Jessica, Kristin, Renee, and Madi for reading drafts and giving him valuable feedback, and Ellis would like to thank Ben, Emi, Bender, Sam, Chaz, Fish, Lowe, Duncan, Ian, Jerald, Josh, and Jackie for giving him advice and help on crafting the art.

And of course, Lev would like to thank Ellis, for being an awesome brother and illustrator, and Ellis would like to thank Lev, for being an awesome brother and for writing the book for him to illustrate.